IN THE SADDLE WITH
UNCLE BILL

WILL JAMES

*They went to enjoying the cool shade
of the quakers that spread over the corral.*

IN THE SADDLE WITH
UNCLE BILL

WILL JAMES
Illustrated by the Author

Mountain Press Publishing Company
Missoula, Montana
2001

First Printing, January 2001

*Tumbleweed Series is a registered trademark
of Mountain Press Publishing Company.*

Library of Congress Cataloging-in-Publication Data
James, Will, 1892–1942.
    In the saddle with Uncle Bill / illustrated by the author.
    p.   cm.
    Summary: While visiting their Uncle Bill on his ranch, two
city kids learn the ways of the western range.
    ISBN 0-87842-428-8 (pbk.) – ISBN 0-87842-427-X (casebound)
[1. Ranch life—West (U.S.)—Fiction. 2. West (U.S.)—Fiction.
3. Horses—Fiction. 4. Uncles—Fiction. 5. Brothers and sisters—
Fiction.] I. Title.
PZ7.J1545 In 2001
[Fic]—dc21   00-011137

PRINTED IN HONG KONG BY MANTEC PRODUCTION CO.

MOUNTAIN PRESS PUBLISHING COMPANY
P. O. Box 2399 • Missoula, MT 59806
406-728-1900

TO YOU

A LOVER OF HORSES AND OPEN COUNTRY

I DEDICATE THIS BOOK

BOOKS BY WILL JAMES

Cowboys North and South, 1924

The Drifting Cowboy, 1925

Smoky, the Cowhorse, 1926

Cow Country, 1927

Sand, 1929

Lone Cowboy, 1930

Sun Up, 1931

Big-Enough, 1931

Uncle Bill, 1932

All in the Day's Riding, 1933

The Three Mustangeers, 1933

Home Ranch, 1935

Young Cowboy, 1935

In the Saddle with Uncle Bill, 1935

Scorpion, 1936

Cowboy in the Making, 1937

Flint Spears, 1938

Look-See with Uncle Bill, 1938

The Will James Cowboy Book, 1938

The Dark Horse, 1939

Horses I Have Known, 1940

My First Horse, 1940

The American Cowboy, 1942

Will James Book of Cowboy Stories, 1951

PUBLISHER'S NOTE

WILL JAMES'S BOOKS represent an American treasure. His writing and drawings introduced generations of captivated readers to the lifestyle and spirit of the American cowboy and the West. Following James's death in 1942, the reputation of this remarkable artist and writer languished, and nearly all of his twenty-four books went out of print. But in recent years, interest in James's work has surged, due in part to the publication of several biographies and film documentaries, public exhibitions of James's art, and the formation of the Will James Society.

Now, in conjunction with the Will James Art Company of Billings, Montana, Mountain Press Publishing Company is reprinting each of Will James's classic books in handsome cloth and paperback editions. The new editions contain all the original artwork and text, feature an attractive new design, and are printed on acid-free paper to ensure many years of reading pleasure. They are published under the name the Tumbleweed Series.

The republication of Will James's books would not have been possible without the help and support of the many fans of Will James. Because all James's books and artwork remain under copyright protection, the Will James Art Company has been instrumental in providing the necessary permissions and furnishing artwork. Special care has been taken to keep each volume in the Tumbleweed Series faithful to the original vision of Will James.

Mountain Press is pleased to make Will James's books available again. Read and enjoy!

The Will James Society was formed in 1992 as a nonprofit organization dedicated to preserving the memory and works of Will James. The society is one of the primary catalysts behind a growing interest in not only Will James and his work, but also the life and heritage of the working cowboy. For more information on the society, contact:

Will James Society
P.O. Box 1572
Elko, NV 89803

WillJamesSociety@yahoo.com
WillJames.org

PREFACE

WELL, HERE IN THE PAGES of this book is the old cowboy again, Uncle Bill, the same cowboy who rode in the pages of a first book under that name and while sort of riding herd over the two city kids, Kip and Scootie, who'd come West to spend the summer in the range country. What the kids done is what any city person would do, and what they learned as they rode by the old cowboy and seen many sights strange to them and asked many questions is also what any city person would learn, young or old, and it's an education that goes well, not only in the range country but would also fit fine in the center of any city. Self-reliance, experience and ability at anything is mighty fitting most anywhere, the old cowboy says.

With this story, *In the Saddle,* Uncle Bill didn't do such a good job herding the kids, but he done a mighty good job hazing a bunch of wild horses, and consequences is he lost Kip and Scootie during the chase, and the "Babes in the Woods" had nothing on the kids as the babes in the big range country.

The kids got to find out plenty more about the bigness of the range country and, as they said, it was sure a lot bigger than any geography ever gave 'em any idea of. But they learned how to take care of themselves in it some, and as you follow their tracks of adventure and then Uncle Bill's thru the book, on the horse range, at cow camps, on mountain ranges, at the home ranch, handling renegade horses and big herds (the same as can be seen and is done right these days), I'm thinking you'll agree with the old cowboy when he says that old Mother Nature and necessity sure don't stinge on education.

Will James

ILLUSTRATIONS

ILLUSTRATIONS

IN THE SADDLE WITH
UNCLE BILL

WILL JAMES

CHAPTER ONE

ALONE, LEAN-FACED RIDER was letting his horse ramble along at a running walk and humming low in tune with the jingling of his spurs as his farseeing eyes squinted under gray and bushy eyebrows to specks and shadows in the big country around him. He'd just been up in the mountains, making a circle thru some of the meadows up there, seeing how the cattle was ranging, if they would be needing salt, and going by signs and rough count of "markers"* as to whether they had been disturbed by any way or was contented and doing well on their high summer range.

The many cattle he'd seen that day all looked mighty well at peace and contented, and that same feeling seemed to be with the rider as he kept his horse along the high mountain ridge which gradually sloped down to the big valley below.

The rider was old but he was lean, graceful and mighty fitting with the action of the good horse under him. His grizzled hair and mustache showed near white against his tanned, weathered face, and when he took off his roping gloves to roll a smoke his wiry hands showed as white as a lady's.

Uncle Bill was the name the old rider was known by in that country, but he had no relatives that anybody knowed

* Odd marked animal.

1

of, and as an all around rough and reckless good cowboy there was few could of tied with him some years before, and now, while riding for the Five Barb 5 outfit he was as valuable in his knowledge of range and handling cattle as any two average younger riders could be.

He'd rode for many big cow and horse outfits scattering from Texas to Montana, and when longhorn cattle was the only kind that roamed the range. After rambling from one outfit to another for many years he'd finally settled down to ride for one outfit steady. That was the Five Barb, and he'd been there since the time the big cottonwoods that was now shading the buildings of the main ranch had been planted and was the height of a man on a horse. Like the big cotton-woods he'd took solid root on the Five Barb range, and even tho he could of made fortunes in the cattle game he was happy to be just what he was, always a cowboy. His wages went for what he wanted, a few days' fun in town after shipping time, range clothes and saddle leather. What money he didn't spend he let ride with the Five Barb and he'd accumulated quite a stake, which he very seldom thought about.

The rambling buildings and corrals of the Five Barb main ranch was surrounded with green meadows and looked mighty pleasant and cool in the mid-afternoon June sun, and as the old cowboy looked the long ways to it from the high ridge he was riding it didn't dampen his good spirits any to know that the ranch was about deserted, deserted of riders, for there was only a couple of ranch hands working there, the chinese man in his cook house and apart from

As an all around rough and reckless good cowboy there was few could of tied with him.

the ranch house, and there was Martha, the good natured and fat housekeeper who took charge of the ranch house for Frank Powers, the owner of the Five Barb.

Frank Powers and six of his riders had gathered saddle horses and rode away some days before to join in with surrounding outfits, and all pooled together for the spring roundup, calf branding and driving back all cattle that'd strayed to other ranges the winter before. Every neighboring cattle owner would be represented in the roundup pool, and each would cut out whatever cattle they owned from the big herds that was rounded up and drive them back to their own range.

Uncle Bill would of liked to went along with Frank, for every cowboy would rather ten to one ride with a roundup outfit than from a ranch. But the old cowboy was more needed at the main ranch, where he knowed every trail and hollow so well, and it was up to him to ride the country around there for the time.

Meadow larks, curlews and a few crickets is about all that made any sound as Uncle Bill rode down into the big flat and on his way to the ranch. He rode by a few bunches of grazing cattle and horses and, as was his habit, took a rough count of new calves and colts and seeing how all was doing.

Not a living thing stirred as he neared the shade of the big cottonwoods at the ranch and all was quiet and peaceful as he rode on to the corral where he proceeded to unsaddle. His horse was tired, but the old cowboy could of caught a fresh horse and rode on without giving that much thought

He rode by a few bunches of grazing cattle and horses.

if such had been necessary. He'd been in the saddle since sun up that morning, it was now late afternoon, he'd had no noon meal and he'd stopped to water only for his horse. He was very much used to going without food or water during the day but if he was around when supper time come he'd do well at that meal.

As he unsaddled he got to kind of wishing that Frank had left a rider with him, not that he needed help with his riding or that he was lonesome, but it was good to "talk cow"* with somebody who savvied, after the day's ride was done. He couldn't get much interested in talk with the ranch hands, the cook didn't count, and as for Martha he didn't know what he could talk to her about, even if he wanted to.

Daggone it, he got to thinking, it's about the time of the year when the kids Kip and Scootie ought to be showing up at the ranch again. He figured that there'd ought to been a letter from 'em long ago as to when they would be coming, but there'd been not a word, and the old cowboy got to kind of wondering.

The kids, Kip and Scootie, which the old cowboy was thinking of was town born and raised, so was their mother, but their dad, Ben Powers, was a range man and none other than Frank Powers' brother, owner of the Five Barb and good uncle of Kip and Scootie.

Ben, even tho a range man, had took to schooling and big education natural-like and that finally brought him to a big eastern city where he went into business and done well. He married and settled down there and raised the two

* Range talk

6

kids, Kip and Scootie, amongst the steel and concrete canyons. But the kids had range blood in 'em and their leaning that way was stronger than their dad's, and since their first summer to the range land, with their Uncle Frank at the Five Barb and old Uncle Bill and all, they took to that land as natural as a duck takes to water. They was throwbacks to the cow country.

Uncle Frank hadn't cared for education, only of the kind that went while in the saddle on the range and amongst stock. There's as much to know at that as there is in any other profession and he'd done as well in his as his brother had in the big city. He'd never married, claiming that he was no home guard and too ornery to expect any female to put up with him. He didn't think he'd even like young-sters, and when he wrote Ben to send his over for a summer vacation at his ranch it was more with the thought that he'd be relieving his brother than anything else. He figured that with his housekeeper, Martha, to watch over them inside and the good old cowboy Uncle Bill to ride herd on 'em outside, he wouldn't have to bother with 'em and he'd be doing his brother a big favor. He had no idea of what fatherly love was like, he didn't know anything about kids, and he figured they was only a big nuisance to everybody and always in mischief, like pups.

Of course, Frank was a little surprised when he met his niece and nephew at the train the first summer they came west. They was only lively and interested youngsters, and well broke, and the show of admiration in their eyes for him and how they listened to his every word kind of got under his hide. But anyway, as soon as he got in to the ranch he turned 'em over to Martha who was as happy to take 'em under her wing as any good mother would be.

That was easy, thought Frank. Next was the old cowboy, Uncle Bill, and it was as he expected when he asked the old rider to sort of herd the kids and see they didn't get hurt. Uncle Bill figured that job to be about as disgraceful as herding sheep would be. At first he took it on like so much medecine, but as he got acquainted with 'em, or that is, the kids got acquainted with him, they soon got under his tough old hide too, and the time soon come when he hovered over 'em like a royal eagle over its young.

Uncle Frank too had got to be at the home ranch more and more often. His riding was with his cowboys most of the time, either at one or another of his cow camps or at roundup wagons, but his long rides got to be shorter, and for no reason that anybody could see he was at the home ranch and, seemed like, only to be in the company of the kids, which he would be right steady, when Uncle Bill wouldn't have them out riding somewhere.

Uncle Bill had took it onto himself to teach 'em some about the cattle game and the range country, how to handle, ride and take care of a horse, how to take care of themselves in the mountains and prairie, how to set camp and cook over open fires, how to rope, read brands and handle cattle, and the kids had proved mighty easy to teach and took on to the life as tho it was theirs to begin with. It was in 'em.

Under the coaching of the old cowboy they learned a plenty during their first summer on the Five Barb range, and they didn't realize until they got back to the big city and school that fall what a holt the big range country had took on 'em. The city people struck 'em as just so many sardines in a can and they got to dodging crowds all they could.

That winter was mighty long. When spring finally come and trees got to budding in the city parks the kids got pretty restless and they'd packed up and was ready to go long before school left 'em free.

They'd had a lot better reception when they got west that second summer. Both Uncle Frank and Uncle Bill had been at the train to meet them and things went on well from where they'd left off the summer before. They got to see some of the roundup and later on they went with Uncle Bill on exploring trips. There was caves deep into the mountains that no known human ever got to the end of, desolate, broken countries where the kids felt they was the first ones there, old rustler and horsethief hangouts, to the elk and bear ranges and then on up above timber line to the tall, sharp rocky peaks where deep crevises held snow and ice the year around.

The kids'd had a great time camping in the open and learned many things. Whatever they seen that made 'em wonder they would ask Uncle Bill and that well experienced old rider always satisfied 'em with his explanations. According to the kids there was nothing the old cowboy didn't know about mountains, prairies and deserts, and they wasn't far from right.

They got to see some of the roundup.

Like the summer before, the second one passed too fast for the kids. There was no holding back time, and the first thing they knowed, after they got back from their exploring trip and rode close to the ranch again it was time for them to hit back for the dreary pigeon-holed walls of the big city. There was tears marring the kids' brave smiles as they parted with the two uncles at the train, and them two tough-skinned range men also got to blowing their noses quite a bit at that time.

"Poor little devils," Frank said, while on the way back to the ranch, "you'd think they was going away to serve a sentence or some such like."

The ranch and the big country looked empty and bigger than ever when Uncle Bill and Frank got back, but there was plenty to do there. The fall roundup would soon be starting and later on there was the preparing for the win-tering of the cattle. There was always plenty of work and the two was *at home* on the range.

That second winter passed even slower than the first for the kids in the city and they was more interested with the figures on the calendar than they was with the ones in their books. But they stuck to their books and studied harder than ever, like as if keeping busy that way time would pass faster. It seemed to by hours but not by days.

Their dad and mother often wondered and talked about their youngsters being so much wrapped up with thoughts of their summers at the ranch and how anxious they was to get back. Their mother figured it was just childish fancy and that they'd get over it when they got older, but Ben hardly thought so, and even tho he'd never mention it, he recognized range blood in 'em and he felt proud and happy at that. He sometimes wished he could go back to the range, even if only for a short while during a vacation he'd take, but his wife liked the beaches and there's where he'd spend his vacations, with her. But some day he hoped that she would go to the Five Barb, with him and the kids and have her see and know some of the range country, then he figured she might like it some, maybe well enough to go there again.

When spring come and the trees budded and then leafed out in the city parks the kids, even more anxious than they'd been the spring before, had long ago got together all the stuff they would need at the ranch and they'd been ready to go within an hour's notice. Amongst their stuff was a package of presents which their dad had bought on a shopping tour with the kids, the presents was for Uncle Frank, Uncle Bill, and Martha.

"I wish you'd come with us to the ranch," says Kip a few days before him and Scootie was to leave. "We'd have a lot of fun together."

"Yes, and you too, Mother," Scootie chips in. "I know you'd like it. I could teach you how to ride and all four of us could go on long pack trips with Uncle Bill or on roundup with Uncle Frank."

Ben only smiled at 'em, like saying he wished he could go with 'em, and his wife noticing that smile, turned to the kids and says:

"I'm afraid we won't be able to this year, children, maybe next year."

"By the way," says Ben to the kids, "I forgot to write Frank and let him know what day to meet you at the train."

The kids looked at their dad and then at one another, both disappointed at first for fear they would have to wait till word reached their Uncle Frank and an answer was received to that effect, but soon their faces broke into smiles, both with the same thought, and they come near speaking at once. But Scootie beat Kip to it.

"We don't need to let Uncle Frank know when we're coming, Dad," she says, jumping up and down all excited. "Let's surprise him—"

"Yes," says Ben, thinking, "but how are you going to get to the ranch from the depot?"

"We—" Scootie started but Kip chopped her off. "I know of somebody who can take us out." Says Kip, "Caldwell at the store."

"Yeh, that's right," says Ben, "and I know he'd be glad to do that too. All right," he decided, "I'll give you kids a note you can hand him when you get there."

So, that's how come that some days later, at the Five Barb ranch house, and as Martha turned from the sink to the stove, that she noticed the kitchen door darken, sudden, she looked, and there astanding in the door, was the smiling and happy Kip and Scootie.

CHAPTER TWO

BACK FROM HIS DAY'S RIDE, Uncle Bill led his horse from the corral where he'd unsaddled him to another corral that was left open to a pasture. In that other corral was a long shed and in the shade of the shed was the saddle and work horses that had come in from the pasture. A glance at them and the old cowboy noticed right away that the horses wasn't all there, two saddle horses was missing, and thinking them two had stayed back in the pasture he climbed up on the shed where he could get a good view. From there he could see all over the pasture, but the two missing ones wasn't in sight.

He came down off the shed and, as a faint hunch came to him, he went into the long stable and to a store room where some harness and saddles was kept. In a corner had been two saddles covered up and put away, and them is what the old cowboy had come to look at. He wasn't so surprised when he looked, his hunch had been right, and both saddles was gone.

But there was more to do to make sure his hunch was right. He went to the cook house and asked the cook if anybody had come to the ranch that day and rode two horses out of the corrals, but trees hid the corrals from the cook

From there he could see all over the pasture.

house pretty well and the cook "no see nobody." Uncle Bill then started for the ranch house to ask Martha, but he'd only got about halfways when she came from the porch, waving her arms, glad all over and hollering.

"The kids are here," she says over and over and all excited. "They got here at noon, Kip and Scootie."

"Yes, Yes," says Uncle Bill, trying to calm her down. "I figured as much, when I seen two horses and their saddles missing. But why didn't the little scampers let us know they was coming, and how did they get here?"

"Well," says Martha, breathing fast, "they wanted to surprise us. They got Caldwell from the General Store to drive 'em out, and when they got here they hardly took time to eat what I fixed for 'em, they couldn't wait to get into their boots and togs and go riding. They said they'd go looking for you and surprise you, but I didn't know which way you went this morning so I couldn't tell 'em where to look for you."

To sort of hide his pleasure of the kids being at the ranch once more, the old cowboy turned and went back to the corrals, but not until after he'd found out from Martha which way they'd rode. He figured he'd do a little surprising himself and catch the kids in the act of looking for him.

He was going by the bunk house, on his way to the corrals, when thinking of ways to surprise the kids good, he happened to glance at a pile of rubbish and a piece of old hair mattress that was there, and he smiled as an idea came to him. He picked out a few tufts of the grayish hair, went to the cook house, and there he hurried the cook to mix up a batch of sticky paste. The cook didn't know what to think, but the old cowboy just grinned at him, told him to hurry up and ask no questions.

In a short while, Uncle Bill had sorted out some likely hair, pasted it on his face, shaped it to a good beard, clipped it into shape with the scissors and then went to the bunk house and changed to some clothes the cowboys had left behind. He even changed his light gray hat to a black one, and when the disguising was all done he figured he would sure pass as anybody but himself. And like the laughing chinese cook remarked as the old cowboy went by, "You lookee like somebody, I don't know what."

That suited him fine. He grinned as he went to the corrals, saddled a fresh horse and rode on the trail of the kids. He was careful as he rode so that when the kids turned to come back to the ranch they wouldn't be the ones to see him first. He rode pretty well in the foothills, amongst scattering pines and where he could look down on the valley, and it was a good thing he done that, for, after riding a few miles from the ranch and getting up on a low ridge, he seen two saddled horses under a lone pine at the point of the same ridge he was on, and sitting in the shade of the tree was the two kids, not over a quarter of a mile from where he was. They hadn't seen him, and he figured they was sure watching for him.

The old cowboy prepared and got all set for his surprising them. He pulled his hat brim well down over his eyes, gave

He seen two saddled horses under a lone pine.

himself a good look over and then rode on, keeping well hid and to make a sort of half circle, and when he would show himself it would look like he'd come from most any direction excepting from the ranch.

He was still hid in the pines when he turned his horse and rode to where he would be in plain sight of the kids, and when he did the kids, not being able to tell who it was at that distance and thinking sure it was Uncle Bill, jumped up, hollered, and getting on their horses rode on a high lope towards him.

They was so glad and excited at the thought of surprising and seeing the old cowboy that they was pretty close to him before they figured they'd made a mistake and stopped their hollering and laughing. They looked very disappointed as they slowed their horses and kept their distance. They eyed the strange-looking rider, and finally Kip managed to say, "Howdedo, Mister." Scootie only nodded. She didn't know whether to apologize for running up to him and hollering the way her and Kip did or what to do.

The bewhiskered Uncle Bill grinned to himself as he watched the kids' expressions from under his hat brim. He hardly expected his disguise to work so well.

"Hum," he grunted. "Well, where did you youngsters come from?"

"We're from the Powers' ranch," says Kip. "We're looking for an old cowboy called Uncle Bill. Do you know him? Did you see him?"

"Uncle Bill? . . . Hum," says Uncle Bill himself. "Sure I know the old reprobate, did that old horsethief get lost?"

The old cowboy had to grin plenty more to himself under his false whiskers as he watched the kids' expressions when he called himself the bad names. They was pretty peeved.

"No, Uncle Bill would never get lost," says Kip, red in the face. "We're looking for him and wanted to surprise him."

"You couldn't surprise that old buzzard. He's most likely at the ranch right now, with his feet under the table and making a hog of himself. . . . Come on, let's ride to the ranch," Uncle Bill went on, "I'll bet that's just what he's doing. I'm going that way anyhow."

It was getting late, and the kids started back with the would-be stranger. They didn't care much for his company on account of the way he talked about Uncle Bill, and they kept quiet and rode pretty well by themselves.

The old cowboy, noticing that and knowing the reason, seen how they sure didn't like anything said against "Uncle Bill" and realizing how much they really thought of him gave him a queer, proud and happy feeling. Then he got kind of sorry for the way he spoiled the kids' fun at surprising him, and thinking of a way to cheer 'em up he decided he'd pull off his whiskers and hat and have a good laugh with them.

He was about to start pulling off his whiskers when Kip rode closer to him and begin to speak.

"How long have you known Uncle Bill?" he asks.

"All my life," says Uncle Bill, feeling that something was coming. He kept his whiskers and rode on, waiting to hear some more. He figured he'd best not call himself any more bad names and be more pleasant then he might hear plenty more.

After a while, Kip went on and he still sounded peeved.

"You couldn't know him very well or think much of him," he says, "or you wouldn't call him the names and speak about him the way you do." Kip was started. "I'll bet he's a lot better cowboy than you are," he went on. "A lot better roper and rider too, and he doesn't slouch in his saddle like a sack of potatoes either—"

Scootie didn't say anything but she was right there to back anything Kip said, and when Uncle Bill heard all and then looked at the peeved faces he was so surprised that he come near giving himself away. He turned his head, and for a while he didn't know what to say.

After a spell, and like wanting to square himself, he begins to speak.

"You kids don't want to take me too serious," he says. "Sure, Uncle Bill is all right I guess but that's just my way of talking about him, kind of joking like."

"Well," Scootie finally speaks up, "I don't think it's very funny."

The old cowboy figured he was in bad. He'd only talked against himself to make his disguise all the stronger, and now he thought it best to keep in his disguise for fear they'd be peeved at the joke he'd played on 'em.

As the three rode on, the kids gradually lost their peevishness and begin to talk about the Five Barb ranch, then Uncle Frank and then, as they went on to talk about Uncle Bill, the old cowboy's ears begin to burn. For the way they talked about him he was nothing short of a bow-legged guardian angel on a horse, a riding and roping wonder, wise as an owl and gentle as a dove, heart of a lion and great as God, and as that went on and on he got more and more uncomfortable in his disguise, and having to take in all the good things that was being said about him he was more than ever hoping that his disguise held good and that he wouldn't be found out. That would spoil everything.

Being careful not to make the kids peeved any more he even had to agree with 'em when all so much good was said about him, and when one time thru the conversation they asked him what his name was there was nothing for him to do but make one up, and right quick.

"They call me Magpie Jim around here," he says, pulling up his shirt collar and pulling down his hat brim, "that's because I'm just a jabbering old fool I guess."

"I don't think you talk so much," says Scootie.

"No," says Kip. "I think you're all right."

It seemed like the kids had forgiven and was beginning to like him, and that made him all the more uneasy. The short distance to the ranch seemed mighty long right then, and to cut out as much conversation as possible and make the time shorter he says to the kids:

"It's getting late and I'm getting hungry. Let's lope along."

The sight of the ranch looked mighty good to Uncle Bill. The three went to the corrals, and as Kip got off his horse to unsaddle he happened to notice the brand on Uncle Bill's horse.

"Why, that's a Five Barb horse you're riding."

"Yes," Uncle Bill got nervous. "I just borrowed him for a few days." Then as he started for the cook house without unsaddling his horse, he says, "I'll be riding on after I get something to eat. I guess you'll find Uncle Bill at the ranch house with Martha and waiting for you."

He went up to the cook house and from there he hurried on to the bunk house. He hurried some more with getting the disguise off, the paste the cook had made sure stuck well and it had to be soaked a considerable before it would come off clean. Once looking like himself and in his own clothes again, and making sure the kids had gone to the house, he rushed back down to the corrals, there was more evidence there which had to be got rid of, the horse he'd rode and left saddled. He hurried for fear the kids would run back to the corrals, soon took his saddle off and put it away, then led the horse to the other corral and slapped him on the rump and out to the pasture.

He took a long breath as he watched the horse lope out to join the others, and to look at him as he turned and started for the house anybody would think that he'd just come in from one of his ordinary rides. The same old Uncle Bill, and sure a contrast from the tramp rider, Magpie Jim, as he'd disguised and called himself.

*He took a long breath as he watched
the horse lope out to join the others.*

He was on his way to the ranch house when he heard some hollering, and looking up he seen the kids running to meet him. He hadn't had any too much time unsaddling and turning his horse loose, for they was headed back for the corral to look for him.

Saying they was pleased to see the old cowboy would be putting it sort of tame. He was just as happy to see them, but he felt a little guilty for the trick he'd played on 'em, and he was still scared to be found out any minute. He was glad that the cook was the only one who knowed about his disguise, and he'd be sure to warn him to keep quiet on that subject the first chance he got.

There was a lot of talk going on amongst the three, the kids done most of the talking and stumbling over one another's words as they went on to tell about many things from the time they left the ranch the fall before and how glad they was to get back.

Their talk was interrupted by Martha who called 'em to eat. "Supper has been waiting and it'll be getting cold again," she says. "Come on children, and you too, Uncle Bill."

What the old cowboy feared came to a head while all sat at the table. The kids, talking on at a fast pace and too excited to pay much attention to their filled plates, of a sudden begin telling of an old rider they'd met that afternoon and was called Magpie Jim. They asked Uncle Bill if he knowed him.

The old cowboy was sort of prepared for that question, and wanting to bury that Magpie Jim for good so there wouldn't be no more questions asked from the kids or anybody else about him he had to be a little careful as to how he answered.

He chewed on a hunk of meat for a spell, then he shook his head and says, "No, I don't know of no such feller by such a name. He most likely was some grub line rider or some old neighbor having a little fun with you."

"Maybe he's in the cook house now," says Kip. "He said he was going there to get something to eat before he rode on."

"Yes," says Scootie, "let's go see."

"Now," Martha chips in from the kitchen door, "you children sit still and finish your supper. That Magpie gentleman'll keep, and Uncle Bill can see him later."

That suited Uncle Bill fine and he was glad to notice that Martha had no suspicion of him. When supper was over he told the kids to start on down to the corral and that he would go to the cook house and see about this Magpie Jim. There he explained to the cook about the disguise and that chinese man thought it was a good joke. He said he savvied when he was told to keep quiet about it and that he wouldn't say one word.

Everything had worked out fine, and when he went to the corrals, and Kip and Scootie remarked that Magpie Jim must of rode away on account of his horse being gone, that all sort of clinched things and Magpie Jim seemed to be well on the way of the forgotten.

"But how is it he was riding a Five Barb horse?" asks Kip as a last word.

"Well, I don't know," says Uncle Bill, sure enough puzzled as to how to answer. "Maybe he borrowed him from your Uncle Frank at the roundup camp, or maybe it's one of the horses your uncle sold a couple years ago."

Kip and Scootie still wasn't quite satisfied about that Magpie Jim. There was something with their thoughts of him which didn't set just right. The way he'd kept ahiding his face while they'd rode near him, and how he'd never looked at 'em while he spoke, and most all about him had made 'em suspicious, specially now, after he'd gone so quiet like. They didn't suspicion anything bad about him, there'd just been something about him that'd made 'em wonder and they couldn't figure it out.

The kids hadn't been on the Five Barb ranch and range for two good summers without learning about the life and the people. Their keen eyes and minds had never let anything slip by without being noticed and figured out, and with Uncle Bill drawing their attention to things they might not of noticed, his explaining, his telling of happenings and coaching them in most of their every move they'd fast caught on and got to where they couldn't be called greenhorns no more. Of course they still had a plenty now to learn but as Uncle Bill often said there's always plenty more to learn for any man in the range country, and the more he learns the more he realizes how much more there is to know.

But the kids had a good start at that and was fast taking holt on things. They was growing with the habits of the range country, more than they realized themselves, and now, starting on with their third summer they'd store up a heap more knowledge that no other life afterwards would ever make 'em forget. They was at a good age now too. Kip was twelve and Scootie was only a year older, and their minds was wide open to all they seen and heard, and none of what they took in was from imagination or thru wild tales, for there was no need for such on the Five Barb range.

CHAPTER THREE

THERE WAS NO SUCH FEELING as "just another day" when the kids woke on the early morning of the day after they got to the ranch. The few mornings before they'd been on a train, and for months of mornings before they'd been surrounded by thick walls, high up in an apartment where the view of tall man-made peaks was all that could be seen thru the heavy and smoky atmosphere. They even made the light of the morning sun shining on 'em look as tho it was man-made, like a powerful electric light. To get to the earth the kids had to come down an elevator and go many blocks, to a park. And even that seemed artificial, for the grass growing there was not the natural grass, it was from imported seeds, and the moisture that made it grow didn't come direct from the rains but from a sprinkler system. It was sure enough pretty, and a mighty welcome sight in the big city, but, as Uncle Bill would of said, it had no guts.

With the kids' first morning on their return to the ranch there was quite a contrast greeting their sight as they first opened their eyes and they had to blink a few times, like to make sure they wasn't dreaming. The first sound that came to their ears, faint at first, was the chirping of hundreds of birds in the big cottonwoods and shrubbery. No sound of elevators, or ash cans being throwed on the sidewalk. There was the low, far away beller of a range bull, the squawling of cayote pups, the drumming of grouse, the cooing of doves and the songs of meadow larks and wild canaries, all from far and close and soothing to the ears.

Cool, clean air breezed in thru the open windows of the log-walled rooms, and as the kids looked out their windows the view of long distances of rolling, green hills which run in ridges to timbered mountains and then to snowcapped peaks. Mountains and peaks full of color and alive in the morning sun's rays. There was no heavy haze over the land.

Kip let out a holler, Scootie answered. They jumped out of their beds and hit the floor at the same time, a couple of steps straight out of their rooms and they was on good sod, with native grass on it. Of course, Martha would sprinkle that grass around the house once in a while but that would seldom have to be done until late summer. On the lawn was a big tub of cold spring water and there's where they splashed their faces, while the morning sun was shining on 'em.

At the kid's first holler, Martha stirred the stove, put in a few sticks of wood, and soon the griddle and pan was hot again, and the coffee simmered strong. When the kids was dressed and run to the kitchen their breakfast was ready and steaming hot. There was no fruit juices on the table, the closest that come to that was stewed prunes and, as

Martha explained, the rollicking around they'd done out in the air, in the sun and while splashing water on one another would about take the place of fruit juices.

They had to eat their breakfast alone that morning. Uncle Bill'd had his at the cook house some hours ago. But even tho Martha kept the kids company they was in a hurry to get to the corrals, and their good appetites and Martha's good breakfast is about all that held 'em at the table.

Down at the corrals, Uncle Bill was busy fixing some extra saddles such as the ranch hands used once in a while. He was working on a stirrup leather with marlin spike and latigo strips when he heard the kids coming, and right then he figured a big day was started.

"Well," he says, grinning at 'em as they come near, "I see you don't want the worm."

"What worm?" asks Scootie.

"You've heard that it's the early bird that catches the worm, ain't you?"

"Yes," Kip chips in, understanding, "but it isn't so late."

"Too late to catch a worm anyhow, so you'll have to do with a horse."

"Fine," says Kip laughing. "I'll get my rope."

"You can get your rope if you want," says Uncle Bill, "but don't you go swinging any big loops around the corral and jam the horses all up. We don't want no horses with barked hips nor lame."

"But I was pretty good at roping before I left last fall, and I've practiced a little since."

"That's all right, but you'll have to do better than you did last fall before I'll let you rope any saddle horses. Practice up on a corral post for a while first and let me see what you can do."

Kip got his rope. It had been pretty well used the summer before, was limp and had about as much life as a dish rag, and when he made a few throws with it the loop spread with about as much grace as a dish rag. There was no good catches made, and it was plain to see that a new rope was needed to start the summer with. Scootie needed a new rope too, for she'd also used the life out of hers.

"You can get your rope if you want," says Uncle Bill.

So there was nothing for Uncle Bill to do but go to the commissary, cut two lengths out of a bale of hardtwist, coach the kids in making hondos on 'em, stretching 'em, and then they was ready for the many loops and throws that would be made.

"But I don't think I'll ever want you kids to rope at broke horses in a corral," says Uncle Bill. "I seldom do that myself unless the horse I want won't let me walk up to him. Roping 'em makes 'em run around too much, crowding and stepping on and bruising one another's heels. In a corral where there's only a few horses it's best to single out the horse you want away from the others and then walk up to him on the left side, either with your rope or bridle in your hand. Most of our broke horses will let you walk up to 'em once they're singled out, and even the ones that are not gentle or well broke can be walked up to, if a feller has a little patience, knows horses and handles himself right. There's quite a knack to walking up to a spooky or half broke horse, and that comes only thru plenty of experience with handling horses."

Being he was on the subject, Uncle Bill went on while he finished mending the saddle, the kids was sitting on the ground close by, watching him and fingering their new ropes.

"Of course," he says, "when there's many horses in the corral and many cowboys wanting to catch theirs then each horse wanted is roped, for there's usually too much going on and it's hard to single out any one horse at a time out of a big bunch.

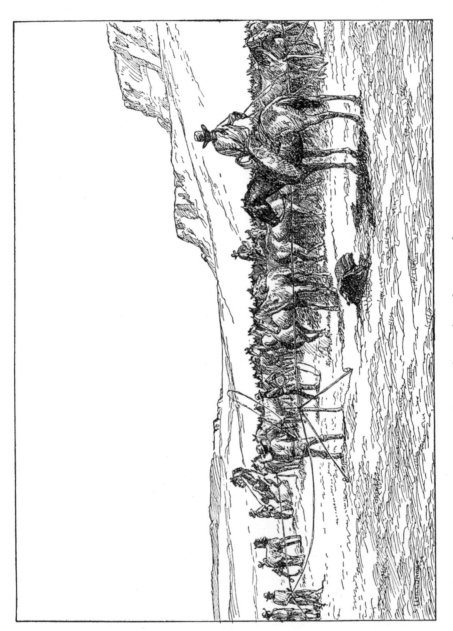

The usual corral used on roundup.

"Like when on roundup. The usual corral used then, such as you seen last summer, is only a two-inch rope cable stretched around into the shape of a round corral, raised about three feet off the ground with stout forked sticks for the cable to rest on, and there's a length of rope from the cable at each stick which is stretched and pegged down on the outside and holding the cable tight all around. Of course such a corral wouldn't hold any horse that wanted to break thru, it would be hard to hold only a few head in such a corral, and what does hold 'em mostly is the company in their own numbers, like with the roundup outfits where the 'Remudas' or 'Caviadas'* is made up of from fifty to two hundred saddle horses. There the wildest ones can sort of hide amongst the gentler ones, and if they do come near the cable that will check and spook 'em back amongst the thick of the bunch. The gentler horses will seldom try to go over or under the cable, for to a cowhorse a suspended rope is something not to be crossed.

"You've noticed too that there's always a few riders around the corral, and if some horses broke thru they'd soon be brought back and they'd want to get in the bunch again, for there's something about a remuda, the company of many and the bells that few horses care to leave once they're a little used to it. The few that do are what we call Lone Wolves, they're the kind you see by themselves on the range, even when they could be with other horses.

"There's seldom more than two cowboys roping at the same time in any kind of a corral, and with the single

* Spanish for big bunch of saddle horses.

cable corrals like the ones used on roundup and which can be let down, coiled and then set up again at every camp the cowboys often rope from the outside. That's sometimes because there's too big a remuda, or too many wild and unbroken ones in it, and if a roper was to go inside and show a loop the horses would crowd against the cable, the pegs holding it would pull out and the roper would soon find himself without a horse inside the flattened corral.

"Every cowboy ropes his horse while on roundup, even tho gentle 'night'[*] horses which could maybe be walked up to. But the horses are well used to that, and the quick and quiet way the loop settles over the head don't flustrate them much.

"But most cowboys sort of quit roping their saddle horses when they settle down to start on some little outfit of their own, then, like anybody else, whatever they own seems to be worth more. They handle their cattle easier and take more pains with breaking their horses. They won't rope 'em any more than they have to because roping spooks 'em and it takes longer to gentle 'em. So, soon as they can, they'll break the horse to stand while being walked up to.

"Some riders 'whip-break' their horses, but mighty few do that. I've never whip-broke one myself, and if I was to buy one that is whip-broke I wouldn't give two bits extra for that." Kip and Scootie perked up their ears some more as Uncle Bill went on. "What we call whip-breaking," he says, "is taking a horse in a round corral and making him

* Horses used on night guard, to hold herd.

face you by stinging his rump with a whip or the end of a rope every time he turns away from you. There'll come a time when, as his rump begins to burn, he'll turn towards you and if you back away each time and drag your whip or rope to the ground he'll get to understand what you want him to do, and in time he'll come up to you as you snap your whip. Later on, if he's well broke at that he'll leave the other horses the minute he knows you want him and all you'd have to do would be to slap your bridle reins or rope against your shap-leg or boot top.

"But I've never seen a whip-broke horse yet that could be depended on to come to you when out grazing, and, if anything, he'll be harder to walk up to than the gentle horse that's not whip-broke, for the only reason he comes to you is on account of the fear of the lash on his tail bone, and he's plenty wise enough to know that when he's out grazing he can easy get away from you.

"So if whip-breaking a horse comes of no good while he's out grazing and he'll come to you only when in a corral I sure don't see no sense to taking the time and pains and aggravating a horse to do what's against his nature. A horse is not like a dog, he's independent and few but barn-raised pets care to be close to a human."

"Is it hard to whip-break a horse," Kip breaks in, "and does it take long?"

"No, it ain't so hard to do, and it don't take so long, only a couple of hours a day for a few days but a feller's got to know horses or he'll make daggone fools out of 'em and so they couldn't be caught only with a loop. Then, if a horse is whip-broke he's got to be reminded of that every so often too. . . . No, sir, you can have your whip-broke and all your trick-broke or gaited horses. I'll walk up to mine in the corral, or rope 'em there and if a horse knows cattle and trails well I sure wouldn't want to spoil him by teaching him any useless tricks."

The old cowboy had went on fixing the saddle as he talked, and now, done with the saddle, he stood up and took it back in the saddle room. In a few minutes he came back packing his own saddle, and laying it on the ground he grinned at the kids and says, "Well, youngsters, now that you've got your new ropes and had your talking to what do you say we put words into effect and catch us some horses?"

That was more than agreeable with the kids, and even tho they wished they could use their new ropes in doing that, they'd had their lesson on that subject, and, with Uncle Bill, they seen it was best to walk up to their horses. They would practice their roping on calves and posts, and some day, as Uncle Bill had hinted, he would let them try their hand at roping some unbroke range horses when some was run in the corrals. "But," he'd said, "you'll first have to learn how to hold an animal and keep your rope slack from under your horse's feet or from around your neck, and that will take time. I'll let you practice on calves for a starter, and when your Uncle Frank comes back from the roundup and we'll be branding the calves around here you'll both have a chance."

"Are you going to take us to the roundup this year?" asks Scootie.

"Well, I don't think so. You see I have to ride this range around here while your Uncle Frank and his riders are away. The roundup started earlier than usual on account of the mild spring this year and I expect it will be over in less than two weeks now." Then seeing some disappointment in the kids' faces, he went on, "But if your Uncle Frank is not back in about a week we'll ride over and meet him on roundup and help him drive the cattle when he starts back. How would that be?"

"That would sure be fine," says both Kip and Scootie at about the same time.

"But for the time being you'll have to put up and ride along with me," says Uncle Bill, grinning at the kids, "and I'm not going to try and do any special entertaining either, if you two can't find things interesting enough as they are here you'd better high-tail it back to the city. You've been here for two summers now and you ought to know what you should and shouldn't do, and I'm not going to camp on your trail much to watch you. So go to it, kids, do your best and enjoy yourselves, come with me when you want or do anything else you want. Of course," he added on, "if I catch you doing anything that don't strike me right you'll sure hear from me about it, but I'll always be ready to give you a hand when you need me and also a good word when you do well."

Feeling free to do as they pleased and use their own judgment went fine with Kip and Scootie, that made 'em feel bigger, more confident and able, and not like greenhorns no more. But they liked the old cowboy's company so well, and being he'd told 'em they could go with him when they wanted to they would sure do plenty of that. Everything seemed so much more interesting and clearer when with him, there was nothing they wondered at that he couldn't explain, and specially on their first morning at the ranch they'd sure have to tag along with him.

The old cowboy expected and hoped for that because he'd long ago planned on giving the kids a pleasant surprise on their first day on the ranch that spring, and when they said they wanted to ride with him that morning that pleased him mighty well, but he was careful not to show any such feelings, and he only told 'em that they could maybe be of some help as he was going to ride to the horse range and run in a bunch of horses, remarking that he needed a fresh string of horses. That sounded very interesting to the kids, for they liked to run horses, and range horses would always give 'em a good run.

Uncle Bill pointed out two of the horses which they'd rode the summer before, and according to his coaching they walked up to 'em with only their bridles in their hands, and helped each other at catching only one horse at a time.

Kip was helping Scootie single out her horse so she could walk up to him when he noticed another familiar horse, one he'd seen only the afternoon before, and recognizing him he hollered to Uncle Bill.

"Look," he says, pointing at him, "there's the horse that man, Magpie Jim, was riding yesterday."

Uncle Bill had thought about that horse when corralling the bunch early that morning, but he didn't figure the kids would recognize him or he'd turned him back in the pasture.

"Is that so?" he says. He didn't have to *act* surprised, then he grinned, "you mean that horse *looks* like that other one, don't you?"

"No, I'm pretty sure it's the same horse, same color and size and one left white front foot, and see the dry sweat on his back."

Sure a noticing little scallywag, thought Uncle Bill.

"Well," he says, like to settle things, "I was riding him myself yesterday and I guess that accounts for the dry sweat."

Kip didn't doubt Uncle Bill, neither did Scootie, but they somehow felt they was looking at the same horse that Magpie Jim had been riding. Then, to sort of take their minds off the subject, Uncle Bill stirred the horses a purpose and proceeded to catch the one he wanted.

As the kids went to saddling their horses they soon forgot all about the other horse, for they sensed that Uncle Bill's eagle eye was on 'em and seeing how they was saddling, so they was careful to do as he'd teached 'em and could think of nothing else right then. They done fine, and as the old cowboy watched 'em from the corner of his eye as he saddled his own horse he was pleased they caught on so well again after being away for eight months. Of course they still had plenty to learn about that, but they had the right start, and the rest would come with practice and experience.

He was also pleased that they hadn't seemed to suspicion him with recognizing the horse he'd rode in his disguise of the day before, and as he got in his saddle he was as happy and carefree as the two kids who was on theirs and ready to go.

On the way to the horse range they begin to come to bunches of cattle grazing here and there, and as they rode thru the bunches, Uncle Bill, glancing at some new calves which played and run at their sight he remarked that some was getting pretty big and there'd soon be a fair sized branding of them, when Uncle Frank and his riders get back. Then all the cattle in the low country, which is saved for winter range, would be rounded up and drove high up in the mountains for the summer.

"I guess it's pretty poky for you kids to be riding along with me," says Uncle Bill as the three was riding at a walk, "you'd most likely like to ride fast and have plenty happening along the way, but that's just what's teached me to ride slow whenever I can. I used to ride plenty fast when I was a kid, too fast, and never thought of saving my horse, and then when things happened and there was work to be done with the stock my horse was too tired to do anything with and couldn't head off a sick cow. I'd have to poke along back with no work done and sometimes would have to walk and lead my wore out horse.

"Any kid is apt to ride the life out of a horse. They don't do it to be mean it's only because they don't know any better, but if they do enough riding and have to depend on the horse under 'em to take 'em to long distances and back they soon learn not to run their horses only when they have to, then they have a horse that can run whenever necessary, they could do whatever work they set out to do and not be riding back on a horse that's all in, nor have to leave the horse behind and make the rest of the way afoot."

The old cowboy didn't start on that subject because he just wanted to talk and didn't have anything else to talk about. Fact is he'd figured it as part of his job with herding the kids to tell 'em, and being that he figured the kids would soon be wanting to ride by themselves more he felt that that sure was one subject they should be well told about before they started and so they'd never forget.

"Take like now for instance," he went on. "Supposing we rode fast all the way to where we find the horses we want, our horses would be already tired when we got there, the range horses would be fresh and ready for a run and we do much riding in running and turning 'em the direction we want 'em to go. Of course these range horses won't run so much and we could get 'em to the ranch all right enough but we'd sure be abusing our horses and they'd be mighty tired when we got there.

"Then again, supposing we had to go further to get the horses and them horses was wilder and run faster, our horses would be ready to quit by the time the bunch was turned, we'd still have the long distance back to the corrals and we'd not only be taking the chances of having the horses get away from us but our horses would be too played out to corral the ones we'd brought.

"You kids have never rode really tired horses and I sure hope you never have to, but I have, and I'm here to tell you that there's nothing more miserable, not if you have feelings for a horse. A tired horse tires you, every time he flinches you do, and if you realize the suffering he's going thru at every step you'll be as comfortable riding him as you would sitting on a spool of barb wire.

"Some folks ride a horse with about as much consideration for him as they would an automobile, or less. I haven't seen but mighty few of them kind of folks but I've noticed that with such there's either a lot of vacant space above their ears or else a big lack of experience with horses. I've seen good cowboys get mighty rough with horses, but with horses that was rough on them, and good cowboys are never seen riding poor, weak and wore out horses, for their pride is with the horses they ride.

"Every man who has real use for a horse should realize that that animal is his best friend. The horse will pack him at any speed, any time or place, and work for and with his rider till he drops in his tracks if necessary. Some would go to that end without having to be touched with the spur.

"Of course I'm not saying that when a feller goes out for a short ride he shouldn't break a horse into a lope or a run once in a while. Horses kept in box stalls and needing

I've seen good cowboys get mighty rough with horses,
but with horses that was rough on them.

exercise enjoy that as much as their riders, but that can be overdone too, if too much at one time. Then again some horses might be tired and still act like they're fresh and rearing to go, them is the high-strung and nervous kind and they should be held down.

"With the cowboy, riding for a living, he don't care to ride just to be riding, there must be some work, like with rounding up cattle or horses or something interesting for him to do and a reason for him to ride, and whenever he rides it's with a habit he's formed thru hard experience, to never run a horse unless it's necessary. He might be riding alone on a good feeling and well rested horse but thru that same habit he's formed he's very satisfied to keep his horse to a walk even if he's riding only a short ways, and unnecessary running strikes him as foolish and for them who have a lot to learn about riding.

"Of course he looks at it different when somebody's only exercising or training a horse, but he don't know much about that because out here on the range our horses are out where they can get all the exercise they want, and as for the training that comes with the work in handling the herds. We're sure in the habit of saving 'em for that.

"So don't mind me if I do so much poking along. I know it must be a little monotonous for you kids. But you can ride by yourselves and as you please when you want to, only don't forget what I told you, that a horse has feelings, like any good friends, and that he's not a hunk of machinery."

CHAPTER FOUR

T HE OLD COWBOY realized it was hardly necessary
to talk to the kids about how a horse should be considered while riding him or at any other time. The kids had
natural and great likings for horses, and with their two summers at the ranch, along with the old cowboy's coaching they
got to know the main things there is to know about the handling and caring of the good gentle horses. But Uncle Bill
wanted to keep that impressed in their minds so that when
they rode by themselves they wouldn't hurt a horse in any way
on account they didn't know and which they would be sorry
for later. The horse is a heap more than just something to ride
in the range country. No machinery or animal ever could or ever
will take his place, and the stockman would be mighty helpless without him. So he's looked at and considered as a mighty
valuable pardner in all works as well as pleasures, and the real
cowboy always thinks of his horse before he does of himself.

His talk over with, and well digested by the kids, Uncle
Bill thought of relaxing them a bit, and looking towards
the rough hills of the horse range, he remarked:

"Well, being we're not going to make so much of a ride
today and we'll have some fresh horses for tomorrow I guess
we can ride along some and loosen our joints."

With that, and without spurring his horse, he broke him smoothly into a trot and then a long easy lope. The kids couldn't do that so smooth, for it takes plenty of riding experience to be able to do that well. Their horses broke into a trot with jerks and into a lope the same way. That was on account they slackened their reins too quick and at the same time touched their horses with the spurs. But they'd get onto that as they done more riding, and in the meantime they was happy to be splitting the breeze.

Loping on to where the country sloped up to the rough hills, the horses was slowed down to a walk again. Uncle Bill had spotted a bunch of horses, and as the horses was about out of sight he didn't say anything and thought of giving the kids the pleasure of thinking of seeing 'em first.

Their eyes wasn't trained to spotting range animals at a distance or in rough country as Uncle Bill's, and they'd rode on quite a ways further and when the horses was in plainer sight before they seen 'em. Scootie was the first to see them but Kip was close second and he seen 'em just as she pointed and hollered.

Uncle Bill acted like he'd also just seen 'em. The horses was near a mile away, and when after looking at 'em he remarked that there wasn't any horses in that bunch he wanted, that made Kip wonder and ask.

"But how can you tell when they're so far away?"

"That's easy enough if you know the horses that's on your range. There's three light colored horses in that bunch, one white and two a little darker, which makes 'em grays or roans, but I know they're grays on account they're with the white one, and the whole bunch numbers exactly to one bunch I know. The light colored ones identify it, and I could tell you that in the bunch, the white one is an old pensioned saddle horse, the two grays are three year old geldings and amongst the dark ones there's four mares and three fillies. Them same horses run together all the time like any other bunch. It's not often that bunches split up, and each bunch can easy enough be identified by the odd colored ones, lighter colored stock in a bunch of dark."

"But supposing there's no odd colored ones in a bunch?" asks Scootie.

"Why, that alone would identify the bunch because there's mighty few bunches where the horses are all one color."

That all seemed clear and easy enough, but Kip had more to ask.

"What about when bunches get mixed up, and after they separate again there's more or less light colored horses in one bunch?"

"There's nothing to do then but ride close enough to investigate, and if you know the horses you won't have to ride very close to identify 'em."

"I guess it takes quite a while to know the horses enough so a man can do all of that."

"Not so long for a man that has an eye for stock and remembers 'em like a cowboy has to. A cowboy could see a bunch a couple of times and he would remember that bunch again if he didn't see it for a year afterwards. That's part of a cowboy's work."

Going on and into the rough hills, Uncle Bill spotted two more bunches, and forgetting about wanting to please the kids by letting them see the horses first he pointed to one bunch amongst some scrub pine about half a mile away and says, "There's the bunch I want."

Kip and Scootie had to look long and hard the way the old cowboy pointed before they could see the horses. Then Kip says, "That's no bunch, I see only two horses."

"But I know them two. You can see from here that one is a black and the other is a sorrel. They always run together and with the bunch I want. You'll see the bunch they're with pretty quick, they'll be close somewhere."

And sure enough. Riding up on a pinnacle the bunch was then in plain sight and close to the two Uncle Bill had spotted.

"Now," says the old cowboy, "we've got to do a little manouvering and get on the other side of 'em before we show ourselves. If we don't I'm afraid they'll give us a run for our money and get away into the hills on us, then it'd be mighty hard to get ahead of 'em and turn 'em towards the ranch."

They rode on and kept out of sight thru the scrub pine until they got well above the horses then turned and rode towards 'em at a slow gait and natural like. At the closer sight of the bunch, Uncle Bill sort of got tense, for he seen three head of horses that didn't usually run with that bunch.

Riding up on a pinnacle the bunch was then in plain sight.

He'd seen 'em before and recognized 'em as renegades which could hardly be turned or corralled, and he figured that if the bunch stayed with their lead he'd sure have to ride some before they could be corralled. He wished now that the kids wasn't with him.

He was going to tell them not to try and follow him and for them to take the straightest way to the ranch when the renegades seen the three riders. They whirled and snorted, spooking the other horses, and then holding their tail high they lit into a run for the thick of the rough hills, the rest of the bunch at their heels.

The old cowboy didn't get to speak. He just couldn't let the horses get away, and the second the renegades started he sort of picked his horse up from a standstill and had him on the run in one jump. To the kids it seemed like he'd just disappeared all at once, and they only got a glimpse of him in a cloud of dust before he disappeared around the point of a rough hill.

It all happened so sudden that they hadn't had a chance to think. They wasn't used to take things in at a glance with range stock and decide what to do in a split second. All they knowed is that they'd seen a bunch of horses, then they hadn't, and the same as Uncle Bill they'd disappeared in a cloud of dust.

The kids stared at one another and for a spell didn't know what to do, but there was the dust still soaring in the air, and, Kip, finally realizing that this was what they'd been wanting, laughed and started his horse.

"Come on, Scootie," he hollered, "let's ride."

They started to follow the dust, that was all they could go by and that was enough. The country was mighty steep and rough, there was many places where they had to jump their horses or go around, and steep side hills where a footholt sure had to be scratched for. Then the twisted scrub pines tore at 'em. Once, Scootie come near being brushed off her horse by a limb, and another time, Kip lost his hat. He wasn't laughing when he had to stop his horse to get it.

They rode as hard as they could in that rough country, and it sure wasn't like riding in a nice stretch and where they could see ahead. The dust was beginning to thin, that meant that the horses and Uncle Bill was fast getting away from them and they tried to ride faster. The horses could go faster but the kids didn't care to let 'em in such a rough country, and for their first time they was going as fast as they wanted to, or even faster.

The dust thinned till it was getting hard to see and follow, and they was getting deeper and deeper in the hills. Then finally seeing no more of the dust and knowing it would be useless to try and follow by tracking they stopped their panting horses and looked at one another with the same thoughts in their minds, wondering what to do.

Uncle Bill hadn't thought of the kids when he first started after the horses and trying to turn 'em towards the ranch. The three renegades hadn't wanted to go that way, they'd took a cut for the thick of the hills instead with the others following, and Uncle Bill, thinking he could head 'em off and turn 'em right quick, had rode after 'em till he got to realizing he'd got quite a ways from the kids. He'd rode so fast and was so bound to turn the horses that he hadn't thought of the distance he'd covered, and it'd seemed like he was about to turn 'em at about every hill, so he'd kept on and on finally figuring that he'd just as well stay with 'em now, also thinking that the kids wouldn't try to follow him much and would start back for the ranch. He had no doubt but what they could easy find their way out of the hills and back to the ranch.

But if the kids wondered what to do now that there was no more dust for 'em to follow they had no thought of going back to the ranch. It was early yet, they figured, about a couple of hours before noon, and if they did miss their noon meal that wouldn't be nothing, for Uncle Bill went without that meal most every day. And to be the real range riders they wanted to be they wouldn't let anything like one meal turn 'em back when, as they thought, they was in the middle of their work, or just started.

They talked things over a bit and then decided to keep on riding still deeper in the rough hills. From the dust they'd followed they got a fair idea of the general direction the horses and Uncle Bill had gone, then they seen fresh horse tracks once in a while which encouraged 'em on.

They rode on and on, glancing at tracks and looking up to the sky for signs of dust. They'd covered a few miles in trying to catch up with the horses and Uncle Bill and it looked like they'd have to ride quite a few miles more before they would catch up. The country looked so still and deserted and not a living thing was in sight.

Then, as they was along on a high lope in the bottom of a deep and rocky canyon, and coming to a sharp turn in it they come near falling off their horses which had stopped and turned sudden at the sight, and so close, of the same bunch of running horses which they hadn't been able to follow.

Uncle Bill had finally been able to turn the bunch, and coming down-country as they was in that canyon they was running at good speed, fast enough so that the three renegade leaders come near running into the kids and their horses. At the sudden sight of the kids to within only a few yards the three renegades was so surprised and spooked up that they didn't even snort but just turned like in midair and hit for the steep side of the canyon and back for the deep of the rough hills again, and the gentler horses, confused and sensing danger in the actions of the leaders, also turned and followed 'em on some more.

So surprised was the kids that they could only stare open mouthed as they set their quivering horses. There was nothing they could do anyway, they'd done their damage, showed up at exactly the wrong place and time and turned the horses back and away from the ranch again.

Thru the cloud of dust that was stirred they seen Uncle Bill holding his horse still, for a few seconds, like as if undecided wether it would be worth while trying to turn the horses again or not, then he jumped his horse once more and started after the bunch. He waved and hollered something at the kids as he started but they misunderstood his waving and took for granted that he meant for them to follow instead of going back, and they hadn't understood the words he'd hollered.

The old cowboy didn't look back as he rode on to head off the horses, for he figured the kids would go back to the ranch now and he would pass them after he'd turned the horses and got them to going that way.

Like with the first time when the horses was spotted, the kids was again left behind and as tho their horses was tied. The bunch disappeared with Uncle Bill riding hard to turn the leaders, and in the wink of an eye there was again nothing to follow 'em by but the dust they'd stirred.

But the kids didn't wonder long as to what to do this second time and soon had their horses on the run in trying to follow Uncle Bill and the bunch. High noon come and the dust had disappeared as before, but they rode on, deeper and deeper into the rough hills. Their horses was now getting tired and the kids was fast getting their fill of fast riding, specially in such country, so they finally let their horses slow down to a trot and once in a while to a walk.

Come the time when they begin losing hope of ever catching up with Uncle Bill and the horses, but every rise ahead made 'em want to ride to see what was on the other side. They seen a few bunches of cattle and horses but no sight of the fast running bunch Uncle Bill was after, nor no dust of it nowhere.

He jumped his horse once more and started after the bunch.

At a distance they seen a tall peak, and knowing that from the top of it they could see far in the whole country around they rode towards it. It was middle afternoon by the time they got to the top and begin looking around, and what come to their sight was not at all encouraging. For many miles around 'em was nothing but more of the same kind of rough hills they'd been riding thru, and not a sign by dust or sight of a running bunch of horses anywhere.

The kids got off their horses and dropped the bridle reins to let 'em graze while they looked at every hill and canyon the direction they figured the running bunch and

Uncle Bill had took. As they searched and watched every place for signs they was careful not to let the dragging reins of their grazing horses get many feet away from them, for as Uncle Bill had told 'em, the bigger the distance around you the more you want to make sure of your horse, and about the best place to trust one not to leave you is when he's inside a corral and the gate is closed.

The distance around 'em was mighty big, and the longer they looked at it for sight of running horses in the tangled up scope of rough hills and twisted pines the less hope they got of seeing them, and being they could see so well for so far they finally come to feel sure that the horses and Uncle Bill wasn't nowhere in that country. They looked far beyond the hills towards a big valley which they thought was in the direction of the ranch and they couldn't see no dust asoaring along there either. Finally, Scootie says:

"Uncle Bill must've turned the horses again, and running so fast I wouldn't be surprised if he had 'em at the ranch and in the corrals by now."

"Yes," agrees Kip, sort of downhearted, "and I guess we're just like two turtles trying to keep up with a grayhound when it comes to keeping up with Uncle Bill, when he starts riding."

Then he added on, "I guess we better start for home. We couldn't be of no help anyway, and we sure got a long ways to go."

They got their horses, and as they started down off the tall peak they both, without saying a word as to direction, figured the same way on a short cut thru the hills towards the big valley and where they thought was home. Their appetites was calling on 'em pretty strong by then, but like true cowboys they didn't dare let themselves even think about that. It was only a couple of hours till time for supper and they figured that with the distance they had to go it would be some hours after that and about dark before they'd get their feet under the table and to taking on some of Martha's good cooking.

They rode on thru the rough hills at a fair gait and they noticed as they rode how their horses wanted to turn to the left at every opening instead of going on the direction that was wanted of 'em. They of course figured the horses was wrong or wanted to go back in the round about way which they'd come instead of cutting thru. Then again they thought, as Uncle Bill had once told 'em, that horses will sometimes go for the range they're used to running instead of the ranch where they're rode from. So the kids didn't pay no attention as to where the horses wanted to go but reined 'em on in the direction of where they thought was the ranch.

They wound their way thru the rough hills, and the sun wasn't so far from setting when they come to the big valley which they figured the ranch was on the other side of and close to the mountains there. As they first rode into the valley and got the closer look acrost it the kids begin to get a strange feeling, like as if they was riding into a land they'd never seen before and where there was no telling if

Nothing but big flat and open country to the mountains.

anyone else had ever been there before. The big valley and
the mountains bordering it looked very much the same as
the one the Five Barb ranch was on but there was something
unfamiliar about it. They could tell better after riding on
a ways further, for then they would be past a long ridge
that kept 'em from seeing all of the valley, and if after that
they could see the big grove of cottonwoods at the foot of
the mountains and which would identify the ranch why they'd
be relieved considerable.

Their hearts was kind of up their throats as they rode
on to pass the long ridge, and then, anxious to learn of
what they might or might not see beyond the ridge, they
rode towards it and on top, and as they got on top and
looked at the big country around was when what they'd feared
came true. For the big grove of cottonwoods which they'd
hoped to see and which could of easy been seen from where
they was, wasn't in sight nowhere, nothing but big flat and
open country to the mountains, and all strange. Kip and
Scootie was lost, far away from home, on two tired horses,
and the sun was going down.

CHAPTER FIVE

WHEN UNCLE BILL left Kip and Scootie, and went after the fast running horses the second time to try to turn 'em back towards the ranch once again he realized how far the kids was into that rough and deserted land. He'd waved and hollered for them to hit back for the ranch, which all they'd misunderstood and thought he'd meant for them to follow him instead, and Uncle Bill, being right busy at the time, riding fast and soon getting out of sight of the kids, hadn't looked back, and thought they'd started for the ranch as he'd motioned 'em to. He sort of wondered as to them finding their way back as he rode on, and he figured to turn the horses he was after so as to be on the kids' trail on the way back, then they could follow him and the bunch as best as they could till they was at least out of the rough country and to where they could easy enough find their way back to the ranch.

But the old cowboy had to ride a lot further and harder than he expected before he could turn the horses that second time. It seemed like the gentler ones wanted to run and keep up with the three renegades, for as it is with all good feeling range horses they was always ready to learn new ways of dodging riders, and the three renegades was good teachers at that. Uncle Bill had to bring on many tricks of his own before he could turn 'em, like letting 'em think they was getting away and keeping out of their sight, then, when they'd slow down to a trot and begin to wander in no certain direction he'd get past and above 'em by keeping out of sight thru timber or some adjoining canyon. He'd then show himself to turn 'em, but for a couple of times the wise renegade leaders wouldn't turn, they'd pick up speed again at the sight of him, scatter past him and then they'd get together again and run on.

It wasn't till the horses came up to the head of a long crooked canyon and was pretty well winded that the old cowboy got the leverage on 'em. He'd rode around and was up there ahead of 'em and where he could do most good. His horse was also pretty well winded when he got up there but if all went well it would be down hill run from there on. And all went well. He came out of a grove of quakers above the unsuspecting horses, let out a war whoop, and the gentler horses spooked at the sudden sight of him and turned, heading back down the canyon on a run, and the renegades, confused for the time, lost their leadership and followed.

Uncle Bill didn't waste no time from there on. He crowded the bunch aplenty, but not so close that it would split and scatter on him, and with the down hill run they took to that as the easiest way to get away from him. He had 'em turned and headed for the ranch once more.

But he was now considerable distance from where he'd last seen the kids. Then again, he didn't know which way they'd be taking on their way back to the ranch, but he'd have to take a chance on that. He had to watch the running horses pretty close because the renegades soon took the lead again and every once in a while they'd take to some cuts for the deep of the rough country. The old cowboy sure had to be at the right place at such times or he would of lost the bunch again. With that he kept awatching for the kids every chance he got and specially when he reached the country where he figured they'd be. He rode on, keeping the renegades headed right, past the country where he thought

He had 'em turned and headed for the ranch once more.

the kids might of gone thru, and on till finally the rough country smoothed ahead of him and the horses took to the big valley leading to the ranch. He could see the big cotton-woods of the ranch some miles away, but nowhere was there a sign of Kip and Scootie.

If the horses hadn't needed his steady attention and if they could of been trusted to ramble straight on or stop to graze he would of made a circle and looked for the kids or their horses' tracks and made sure they'd got out of the rough country. But there was no trusting the horses for one second, for in the wink of an eye they'd broke back to where they come from. He'd of course let the horses go mighty quick if he'd thought for one minute that the kids was on their way of getting lost right about then, but he couldn't make himself believe that they might be, for he figured that with their experience with him on many long rides, and with them not being too far in the rough hills when he'd last seen 'em they'd sure find their way back. Then again, even if he hadn't seen 'em and they was still in the hills, he thought sure that they'd watched for the dust the running horses had stirred on the way back and seen it. It could be seen for miles around, and they could easy follow it on out of the hills. (The old cowboy figured 'em too near like himself in experience that way.)

But, as he hazed the horses out of the last of the rough country and out on the open flat, Uncle Bill figured sure that the kids was well on their way to the ranch and away ahead of him. They'd had plenty of time, he thought, and if they rode as he expected they would when by themselves that way they could even be right there unsaddling, or waiting to help him corral the horses he was bringing. And, as he looked on the big flat towards the ranch and seen two bobbing objects come to sight and then disappear, like in some lower country, he figured that right there was the two kids and loping along on their way home.

He kind of forgot about 'em then and put all of his attention on the horses, and they sure needed all of his attention too, for it was about then, and when the rough country was being left behind, that the three renegades begin to act as tho they sure didn't want to go very far on the big flat, and they was sort of getting their second wind to make another break back for the rough country.

Uncle Bill kind of expected that. He'd liked mighty well to've taken them three on in but his horse was getting pretty tired, and if he could head 'em back after another break it would be doubtful if he could get 'em close to the ranch even then. Then the corralling would be a mighty ticklish job and he'd be more apt to lose 'em there than any other place. If he had a fresh horse right then, he thought, as he watched the renegades he'd sure get them in the corral or else make things mighty miserable for 'em on the outside, for such outlaws sure can turn well-behaving range horses into regular ornery ones, like themselves. But, as it was, riding a tired horse he didn't care to try to bring the renegades along or try to corral them. He'd get them some other time, and now that he had the bunch out of the rough hills and where he had a better chance of handling them he figured it best to let the renegades break back whenever they wanted to, and ride hard only to keep the others and head them on to the ranch. He didn't want to run his horse any more than he had to because he'd be taking the chance of not only being set afoot but he'd also be losing the horses he'd set out to get and wanted to bring in.

Once well out on the flat he slowed his horse down. The bunch slowed down too, for they had their run and all seemed satisfied, all but the three renegades, and them three only seemed to get more nervous. They'd run up ahead, and when the bunch didn't follow so well they didn't know whether to slow down and wait or run on. They done that a few times and then they finally broke away and quit the bunch. The flat was too open and the corrals was getting too close.

The old cowboy thought there'd be trouble when that happened and that some of the gentler ones would try to follow them. A few did start to but he was prepared for that and he rode to scare 'em back, at the same time getting the bunch to moving faster again and straight ahead, which all stampeded the three renegades all the more, and the country being left open to them they hightailed it at a speed that none of the gentler horses cared to follow.

The old cowboy watched 'em go, and as he did he decided right there and then that he'd make a special ride to get them some day soon, before they had every bunch of range horses around spoiled as they was. The gentler horses behaved well again after the renegades got out from among 'em and disappeared, and Uncle Bill had no trouble on the rest of the way into the ranch and corralling them.

He was a little surprised after he'd corralled the horses and closed the gate on them and looked thru to the other corrals that neither Kip nor Scootie was around to meet him. They'd sure seen him come if they was at the ranch, he thought, and then he got the scary feeling that they might still be in the rough hills, looking for him, or lost.

He rode up to the ranch house, hoping they was there and taking on some of Martha's cooking. He got off his horse and went into the house, but Martha hadn't seen them, and as she looked at the old cowboy's face she only got worried and begin to ask questions. Uncle Bill first told her to make up a parcel of grub to take along on his saddle, enough for a couple of meals for the kids. He didn't want any for himself, he'd kill his own or go without. Then as she worked on that he gobbled up mouthfuls of cold meat and potatoes and went to answering her questions.

It wasn't many minutes later when he was down to the corrals again, caught up and saddled a fresh horse, turned all the others out in a pasture and then hit out, back for the rough country. The day was fast getting on, and he knowed it would be dark by the time he picked up the trail from where he'd seen 'em last, but he hoped to see the kids before he got that far, maybe on their way back.

He rode hard, keeping a mighty sharp look-out for the kids as he did. The sun was pretty low and he hadn't seen no sign of 'em when he started into the rough hilly country, and it was near dark by the time he come to the place where he'd seen 'em last. He easy enough found their horses' tracks, but a short ways from there them tracks soon mixed up with those of the horses he'd been running, and seeing that they'd been trying to follow the bunch he come to figure that they sure must of went on quite a ways, then trying to keep track of the windings of the horses they'd lost their sense of direction. So, when they stopped and turned to hit back for the ranch, thought the old cowboy, they'd turned the wrong way. He seen for sure now that they'd went and got lost, and being that it was now pitch dark and, of course, couldn't do any tracking and couldn't guess which way the kids had gone Uncle Bill figured that the best and only thing for him to do was to bed down amongst the boulders for the night and start on their trail early in the morning.

He then thought of a spring he'd passed while running the horses that day and being it wasn't so far away he decided to ride over to it, maybe the kids would be there, and if not he could anyway water his horse. He wasn't disappointed not to see the kids at the spring when he got there for he figured they'd rambled on further even if they had come to it.

Being it now was dark and he couldn't do any tracking he thought it best not to go any further that night. He watered his horse then looked up the skyline for the highest timbered hill. There was one that run to a high point on the top of which was a few wind twisted trees and he started his horse for that high place. It was a hard steep climb but once up there the old cowboy seen he was sure enough high. Good bunch grass was up there too. He unsaddled his horse, and to make sure of him he hobbled and side-lined[*] him, then he sized up a likely pitchy tree and lit a fire to it. The tree blazed up like a big torch that could be seen for many miles, then holding his horse so he wouldn't try to run against the hobbles he pulled out his six shooter and emptied it in the air, each shot about ten seconds apart. With the blazing tree that could be seen for so far and then the loud report of the forty-five six-shooter that could be heard for a long ways in case some hill hid the sight of the blazing tree, Uncle Bill figured that would fetch any person to attention for a good distance around, specially a lost person.

That was all and the best he could do during night time that way. The shots, he figured would start the kids to looking if they was to within hearing distance, and then seeing the blazing tree they'd sure think it was him, Uncle Bill, and come to it. All he'd have to do now would be to keep the blaze alive for a couple of hours so that if they started to come they would have time to get to it before it died out, which would keep them from leaving, wondering as to where the fire had been.

The first pitchy tree blazed up good for over an hour, and would burn on the ground for longer, then the old cowboy lit another one, a bigger one, shot five more shots in the air, waited a spell to make sure the tree would burn on good and then fitted a place for his hip in the dry gravelly ground.

[*] Hobbling one front to one hind foot about three feet between.

The first pitchy tree blazed up good for over an hour.

With his head against his saddle he was soon asleep. He would sleep till daybreak (in the month of June that comes mighty early) and then, soon as it was light enough to see he would start on the trail. He hadn't worried so much about the kids. If they didn't come to his fire that night they'd be quite a distance away, but he figured that if he found 'em within a couple of days they'd be all right and the experience would only do 'em good. He felt sure of finding 'em before the end of another day.

But if Uncle Bill seemed to take it so easy about the kids being lost, the kids themselves sure done their share to make up for that. They was worried aplenty, and when the sun went down and night come on them on the bare ridge in the big country they got to feeling mighty all alone in a mighty big world, a lot bigger world than any school map had ever given 'em any idea of. As the last light of the day gave way to darkness in a world so big and empty, they'd given a year's growth to be by Martha's loaded table. A drink of that spring water by the milk house would sure go well they thought, they hadn't had any water or food since that morning, the longest time in their lives, and they'd been riding all day. If only Uncle Bill was with them all would be well, they at least wouldn't have the fear and lonely and helpless feeling they was experiencing. Nothing was puzzling and all went so well when he was near.

They was thirsty and hungry and tired, and their horses was the same. But that didn't worry the kids as much as

what they should do or where they should go. They couldn't
get to realizing of having to stay for the night in the big
bleak country without food or bed. They talked that over
in every angle for a spell and for some way out, but no angle
led to anywhere in their minds, it was all dark alleys, or
dark empty land, and they figured that wherever they'd go
they'd find themselves in the same fix they now was in, for
it'd been a miracle if they'd found food or shelter in that
night's ride.

A cayote barked and howled not far away, another
answered, and that sure didn't help things with the kids
at that time. They had liked to listen to the cayotes howl
while at the ranch or when Uncle Bill was near. It had
sounded musical like and cheerful then, but now it sounded
mournful, lonely and even threatening.

They sat on their horses, like plum dejected and helpless, doing little talking and a heap of wondering. They would
of rode on but they'd come to think that they might only
lose themselves all the deeper and tire their tired horses
all the more, and being also mighty tired themselves is
what finally decided 'em to slide off their saddles and get
down to earth.

"Let's forget it," Kip had said, "and make camp right
here."

Forgetting it meant food and bed, and making camp was
only a borrowed remark from Uncle Bill, for they had nothing
to make camp with. It would be just a stop. They unsaddled,
and as the horses went to reaching for scattering tufts of

sand grass the kids went to figuring of a way to fix them so they could graze thru the night and still not be too far away when morning come. They couldn't picket 'em with their ropes because the grass was too scattering and scarce, and then there was so much brush that the ropes would only get tangled up in it and bind the horse to one place. Hobbles seemed to be the only thing that could be used in that country, and they now wished they'd left the soft cotton rope strands which Uncle Bill had put on their saddles for that purpose, but they'd seemed so useless on account they hadn't needed 'em for so long and they'd took 'em off.

It looked like the only way now was to cut two lengths off their ropes and make hobbles out of that. The hard twist rope would be apt to burn the horses' ankles, but they figured that their gentle horses wouldn't go against 'em much, and tired and hungry as they was they would be glad to graze and cover as little ground as possible. They didn't think about the horses being thirsty and that would cause 'em to drift after taking a few bites of the sand grass. That day's run had been hot.

If they'd been watered that evening they'd be more apt to stay. As it was, an experienced rider wouldn't of trusted 'em with hobbles, but an experienced rider would of found water if there was any, if not he'd rode on till he did or kept his horse close to him till morning come, for its mighty hard on a horse to drift on a long ways looking for water while hobbled, harder on him than going without it and being tied up all the night. Of course a horse has to eat and drink, and an experienced rider will look out for that, and if he gets in a fix like the kids was he'll ride on, if he has hopes of finding water. If not he'll keep his horse close till daylight and when he can see by the lay of the land where water could maybe be found. After watering his horse he'll then give him time to graze and rest up, and he won't be afoot.

The lengths of hard twist rope Kip and Scootie had cut wouldn't make very good hobbles. The kids realized that. The stiff rope wouldn't pull down into a knot that could be depended on to stay, but they done their very best at that in the dark, and when they was thru they felt pretty sure of their job. They was too tired to worry much about that at the time anyway.

They was a little chilly too, for their clothes was light in the cool of the night. A fire would sure go well, they thought. It would not only warm 'em but it would cheer things up all around and drive away the gloomy and desolate feeling they had. It would be good company too to sit by and watch and keep poking at if the night was cold and they stayed awake thru the night. Uncle Bill came to their minds again at the thought of it. He'd told 'em a few times that a person should always pack a few matches, wether that person smokes or not, and to never rely on another person for them, for matches come in mighty handy for many purposes, any time and place. The kids thought of what they'd learned in school about woodcraft and how to start a fire without matches, but all of that learning didn't seem to amount to much right there and then. It was dark, they wasn't in no woods, there was no flint nor moss or nothing that seemed to jibe with what they ought to have. It had all seemed plain and easy enough in the book but this bleak dark land of low scattering brush and gravelly earth was no book, it was raw reality and couldn't be opened or closed as was wished.

But the kids wasn't in near as bad a predicament as they might of thought. Being miles from any other humans for the first time in their lives and lost in that big bleak country, feeling so little and so lost, and realizing there was no one they could go to for help, all more than worked on their imagination and made things seem twice as bad as they really was. They thought of dying of thirst or hunger and pictured themselves wandering half crazy over the desolate country.

They was cold and tired, and the bare ground seemed only a little better than having to stand up all the night. They'd read aplenty of sleeping under the stars with only a saddle for a pillow and a saddle blanket for covering. That had read good while at home and made 'em hanker for such adventure. Now they was having it, a little overdose of it, and they didn't care so much for the adventure. But if they hadn't been lost they'd appreciated it some.

They felt around for a level place in the gravelly ground and layed their saddles so as to use the seat for a pillow, but that didn't seem to work so well, so they layed them on the side, as should be, and then they put their head inside, between the saddle skirts, that way the saddle served as a wind break and the upper skirting kept off cold air from up above.

As for covering, the saddle blanket would have to do in such a case. But another adventure flavor was sort of spoiled there, for the blanket was heavy and clammy from horse sweat, and haired pretty well all over. Kip spit out some hair and remarked that as for sleeping blankets they sure wasn't what they was cracked up to be. Scootie agreed, but for some shelter from the cool night air they would have to do. They just spread the blanket over them as it would go over a horse's back, and didn't unfold it because, as Uncle Bill had told 'em, a saddle blanket shouldn't be unfolded any time on account that after it's taken the shape of a horse's back it would be kind of hard to fold it back the same and without a wrinkle between the folds. A wrinkle is hard to notice sometimes and will often cause a sore back.

There was no clothes pulled off as the kids settled to that night's stay so close to mother earth, they kept their hats and boots on and never thought of taking even their spurs off. Being tired they kind of forgot about their thirst and hunger and lonely feeling. They settled down to accept things as they was and with strong hopes for the next day, when the sun would shine again. There was only one reminder of their predicament to disturb 'em as they begin to doze, and like a "good-night" of the bleak land around 'em, that was the yip and long drawn out howl of a cayote. Scootie raised up at that and sort of shivered, then without any more howdedo she got up, moved her saddle and blanket right next to Kip's and cuddled close to him. After a while both was sound asleep. Two Babes in the range land.

There was no clothes pulled off as the kids settled to that night's stay so close to mother earth.

CHAPTER SIX

A CHEERFUL WARMING SUN peeped over a tall range of mountains to the east and slanted its first rays acrost the big country to the long ridge where huddled the two kids under their saddle blankets. A little lizard skipped up on the saddles and cocked an eye at the two heads, a deer fly buzzed around a bit and landed on Kip's ear, and the day was begun. Kip woke up and raised his head as the fly landed, the lizard scampered away, and then Scootie opened her eyes to stare at the lining of the saddle skirt above her head.

An early morning sun always has a great way of chasing away the gloom and loneliness that might come after the evening sun has gone down, even if that sun has scorched, and brought thirst the day before. There is times, during long and hot and dry spells when a feller sort of dreads to see the sun come up, and that's with the thought of the coming heat for later in the day, but every human and living thing welcomes the first rays of the morning sun.

Kip and Scootie more than welcomed it that morning on the long ridge. The gloomy and desolate look of the country the night before was now bright and promising. There'd be some more adventures to come but with the light of the sun on 'em they felt ready for whatever might come. There was no washing of faces or combing of hair after they jumped up that morning, they only stretched to the sun's warm rays, dusted themselves with their hats and they was all ready for the day, for there'd be no breakfast that morning, but their hunger, like their thirst, didn't seem to be so strong right then as the evening before. They was also pretty well rested up.

It was a good thing that their spirits was up to near average, for as they begin to look around for their horses, and they could see for a long ways from where they was, they didn't see a sign of 'em nowhere in all that big country, and their hearts skipped a few beats. They looked around again very careful and plum up to the deep cuts of the mountains acrost the big flat, and they sighted one bunch then of what looked like horses, but there was too many in the bunch, they didn't think their horses would pick up with any bunch anyway, and then they didn't think they would go that way but towards the ranch. They was lost and had no idea of which direction the ranch layed but they somehow felt it wasn't the way the bunch of horses was.

"Well," says Kip, finally, "it looks like our horses left us and we're afoot."

Scootie squinted far in the distance and nodded. "Yes," she says, "and the only thing I think we can do is cover up our saddles with the blankets and go look for them. We sure can't get lost any more than we are and we can't stay here and die of thirst."

"We better leave our spurs here too," says Kip, "because it looks like a long walk ahead for us. . . . We're sure greenhorns yet," he went on. "We not only turned the horses back on Uncle Bill when he had 'em headed right for the ranch, but we go and get lost, and now lose our horses and here we are, afoot."

The kids looked at one another kind of sheepish like, and then they grinned a little.

"I guess we'd better track 'em down," says Kip as he looked at the tracks where the horses had been hobbled the night before, "that would be the only way we could find 'em."

They zigzagged along with the tracks where the horses had grazed for a while and then they found one hobble, the hard twist rope had come untied. Scootie picked it up and looked at Kip, mighty serious. The kids knowed what that meant. It meant that one horse was free to travel as he pleased, and the other, not wanting to be left behind, would keep up with him. They would be traveling as fast or faster than the kids, and they wouldn't be caught up with until they'd found water and stopped to graze, which might not be till they reached their range, wherever that was. (In good grass country a horse's range covers about twenty miles in length and width. It's where he's born and raised, and he'll go a couple of hundred miles to get back to that range whenever he's free. If he's taken away to some other far away range and gets located there after a while he'll go back to that place too but not as far as he will for his native range.

It's been known of some horses traveling four or five hundred miles to get back to the range where they spent their colt days.)

Uncle Bill had told the kids about the range horse's strong homing instinct, and now that they found the one hobble they felt more than ever afoot, for the free horse would sure hit for his home range and the other would do his best to follow.

That kind of stopped 'em for a while and they wondered what to do, but realizing that they sure couldn't stay where they was they figured that they'd better follow the tracks. There was hopes in them somehow, and they was hoping mighty strong that the horses whose tracks they was following didn't range too far, they also hoped that the hobbled horse would sort of hold the free one back some.

"The hobbled horse will burn himself up pretty bad, I think," says Kip, "if he tries to keep up with the other one."

They hurried a little more as they went, like to catch up with the horses as soon as possible. The tracks went in a pretty straight course from where the hobble was found, and that showed that the free horse sure had a very certain place he wanted to hit for. They didn't go towards the bunch of horses which Kip and Scootie had seen, nor to the rough country they'd been thru the day before and which was the Five Barb horse range. They didn't go the direction the kids thought the ranch might be either, but just the opposite and acrost the big flat towards a low range of far away hills, and as the kids looked at the long distance where they could

And then they found one hobble.

of seen a horse for five miles, and not seeing a sign of 'em ahead they felt some discouraged. But the day was just beginning, it was still cool and they felt they could go a long ways. They had to.

Anxious to at least get a sight of the horses, which would encourage 'em a considerable, the kids walked pretty fast, sometimes even skipping into a trot for a few steps. As they went on that way thirst was fast beginning to call on 'em again, and on that account their hunger wasn't as strong as the day before. They didn't think or talk about their thirst any more than they could help. They was kind of afraid to, for the way the country looked and the direction they was going it sure wasn't promising that they'd get to quench it soon.

They'd gone a few miles from where they'd found the first hobble when what they feared they would find did come to their sight, it was the second hobble. That meant that the second horse was now free to travel as he pleased, and not only that but the worst of it was that the horses couldn't be caught now, for being free that way they wouldn't let the kids get to 'em so a rope could be slipped around their necks. The horses was gentle but they was range bred, raised free on big ranges, and not at all like the barn raised horse that's used to being fed grain and expects a handful whenever he sees a human. The barn raised horse is not independent like the range raised horse is, even his looks and actions are different and he'll most always let a human walk up to him and catch him while loose in the pasture. He'll even come to meet that human sometimes. But the range horse is not that way, and no matter if he's gentle and been fed grain he usually always has his eye for the hills and freedom. Another thing is he's used to being caught only after he's been run into a corral, and he seldom can be caught outside of one unless a rider ropes him from another horse.

Kip and Scootie realizing that felt pretty hopeless as they picked up the second hobble. It had come untied as the first one had. Now they felt afoot for sure, for even if they got to within twenty feet of their horses they knowed they couldn't ever catch 'em, not unless they come to a corral somewhere and that seemed as unlikely in that country as coming to a babbling brook, and even if they'd come to a corral they might have a hard time running them in afoot.

But, as the old saying goes, when there's life there's hope, the kids still somehow found some hopes in the horses' tracks. They'd been made by the horses that'd packed 'em only the day before, and that had some to do with keeping a little of their hopes alive. Anyhow they didn't want to lose sight of 'em, and another thing, as Kip and Scootie figured, them horses would sure be going to water while on their way to wherever they was headed, and by following their tracks they would at least get to that water, which for once in their lives had got to be a mighty precious fluid, a heap more than any faucet had ever given them any hint of.

Uncle Bill had once told 'em that the best way to find water in a barren country was to follow tracks of animals, and them tracks will in time lead to others and then to a plain trail to water.

Water was fast getting to be about as important as the horses with the kids, and they figured that with the heat of the day coming on and with their walking, they'd sure be in misery if they didn't get water before many hours. They traveled as fast as they dared while it was still a little cool, and as they went on and on they got to following the horse tracks more with the thought of the water them tracks would lead to than to catch up with the horses that made 'em.

The country ahead and where the tracks led sure looked plenty promising as to distance but not at all as to any moisture. It looked better either to the left or right, but having belief in the horses' tracks leading to the closest water they stuck to them. They walked on, one behind the other to save dodging around brush as they would by keeping abreast, and once in a while they'd look back at the long ridge where they left their saddles so they could identify it and the country around where they'd come to get them.

It might of been kind of strange for two town raised kids like Kip and Scootie but there wasn't a time when they looked back that way that they once thought of Uncle Bill or anybody being on their trail and coming to their help. They knowed that Uncle Bill could easy enough track 'em but they thought only of how him and Martha would be worried about 'em, and not at all that he might be on their trail. If they had they'd stayed by their saddles, or would of turned back after they found the hobbles and realized how well afoot and far from any place they was.

They figured it was pretty well thru their own ignorance that they'd got in the fix they now was in and it never came to them to expect any help to get out of it. If help came that would be a big surprise, and the two being so self reliant that way sure must of come from the generations of range and pioneer blood that was their father's.

That showed on 'em strong as they walked on, thirsty and weary and nothing encouraging in sight to cheer 'em. They'd got peeved and disappointed as things went wrong but they never waited nor whimpered and there was no sign of quitting in their system, not even if they was discouraged, for even then they found hopes in round about ways and all was believed as some promising until the worst sure enough proved itself.

The way the horse tracks led, the kids figured that the closest water must be in the low range of hills which they'd been hitting for since sun up that morning. They'd been walking about four or five hours, the sun was now hot and it looked like they still had about ten miles to go before they would reach the low hills, and maybe water. They had no more thought of food for the thirstier a person gets the less hungry he feels. From the closer look of the hills they could now see that they was pretty well covered with scrubby timber. The hills was bigger than they thought too, for, at first, and on account of a rise in the big flat they hadn't been able to see the bottom of 'em. They could now also see quakers in the draws, and that was a good sign of water, specially for that time of the year, and then they got to thinking that there might be corrals somewhere too and so they could catch their horses if they ever caught up with 'em. But there still was no sign of their horses in the distance. They sure would hate to lose their horses, for they not only needed 'em but they figured that losing 'em would also go against 'em in Uncle Bill's opinion. It would be bad enough to've got lost themselves.

They sat down to rest for a spell in the little shade of a tall brush, the air was still and they started to talk a little, Scootie once remarking on what a change it now was, sitting, lost and afoot in the big country so far from the big city they'd left just a few days ago where comfort and everything could be got by only pressing a button. Kip remarked that an ice cream soda sure wouldn't go bad, and that sort of wound up the talk on the subject. But it did bring something else to their minds which they often read and wondered about and that was that when men in the desert got real thirsty they would put a couple of pebbles in their mouths and waller 'em around with their tongue. That would somehow stir up saliva and hold the thirst and swelling of the tongue down.

Now was sure a good chance to try that, they thought, they was plenty thirsty enough and they noticed as they talked that their tongues was beginning to swell a little. They each picked up two pebbles, placed them in their mouths and started walking again. After a while the pebbles did stir up some saliva and relieved the thirst a little, but most of the saliva was used to spit out the grit, and later on the pebbles was also spit out. They didn't seem to help much and the kids was afraid they'd only make 'em thirstier.

The sun kept a getting higher and hotter, their thirst kept a getting worse, their feet begin to lag and burn and at times the hills they was headed for seemed to get farther away instead of closer. It was one of those hot June days, and to the kids it seemed all the hotter on account of their thirst and having to walk.

The next few hours, as the sun went up to its peak and then started to circle down again, was the longest and was filled with more suffering, downheartedness and struggling than any hours they'd ever put in their lives. Of course they hadn't lived so long as yet and had never suffered any to speak of, but their experience in that bleak stretch of country would be the one that would stand as far above the worse of any that might ever come their way later on, even if the later experiences would really be twice as bad.

As they trudged on, sort of aimless, it got to seeming that they was seeing horse tracks everywhere they looked, even up in the skies, for they'd kept so close a watch of the tracks they'd been following in the hot sun that they was sort of printed in their minds, and then, when about middle afternoon, and coming to where the horse tracks on the earth turned sharp and in another direction from where they'd been heading, the kids went right on and quite a ways before they noticed that they'd lost 'em.

But they was up a draw of the timbered hills by then, the hills they'd been seeing as they watched ahead for the horses since that morning, and looking up the draw about half a mile and to where it narrowed they seen a big grove of quakers. They was a little worried about losing the horses' tracks and they'd of went on to find 'em, but they noticed a corral sort of hid amongst them quakers and that give a strong hint of water being close somewhere around there, for corrals are very seldom built where there's no water near.

The shade of the quakers alone looked mighty cool and inviting, and with the sight of the corral and the thought of water, that decided 'em to forget about the horses' tracks for the time being and investigate around some. It was pretty hard walking up that draw, for they was very tired and suffering from thirst, and they staggered some as they made their way up the loose gravelly dirt and around big boulders. But they was cheered up some at the sight of a plain trail and the many fresh hoof marks that was on it. There sure must be water up there, they thought, looking towards the grove.

They shuffled on a little faster, then as they got nearer the corral the trail itself got to be moist, like from the drippings of wet hoofs that had gone over it. They hurried on some more, neither saying a word but both with the same high hopes as they followed the trail. The trail got damper and damper and led straight for the corral gate. It was a little muddy there at the gate but dry inside the corral, all but to the far side, and there was a trough, full of clear water and running over. A grooved length of quaker stuck thru the corral bars just far enough to allow what little water it carried from a close spring to drop inside to a big hollowed cottonwood log which made the trough. There wasn't much water falling into that trough at a time, just a little stream about the size of a very little finger, like Kip's or Scootie's, but no big waterfall or deep pool could of looked any better to the kids right then than that clear little stream.

At the sight of the trough and the little stream of water the kids rushed, but once there they both, at the same time and with the same thought, went to warning one another and to go slow with the first few swallows. For they'd heard and read of the dangers of drinking water too fast after a long thirsty spell. Cold water as it was from that spring was all the more dangerous, and even tho taking only a few sips at a time and waiting for a spell before taking any more was hard to do, the kids sort of helped and watched one another on that, and while waiting for a reasonable time to take on more sips they went to enjoying the cool shade of the quakers that spread over the corral and all that was moist and green around 'em.

CHAPTER SEVEN

As KIP AND SCOOTIE slowly quenched their thirst and rested their tired bodies in the shade they begin looking around 'em in wondering if they'd come to any place where anybody might be living somewhere close. The first thing that drawed their attention as they sat inside the corral was the gate they'd come in from. It was hung different than any other corral gate they'd ever seen. It looked like any other gate, all excepting with the end pole where it closed. That pole was long and stuck well up in the air, and at the top was a long heavy smooth wire which stretched high above one side of the corral and strung out thru the quakers. It looked like a wire to pull the gate shut with from a distance and out of sight, and from that the kids figured that the corral was used as a trap for stock that was hard to corral and the gate would be pulled closed on 'em when they came inside to drink.

The little stream that run into the watering trough was enough to water only a few head of stock at a time and what run over sunk in the gravel inside the corral, no water run out of it. It was a water trap such as had been described to the kids before, only this one wasn't for the wildest of stock, for if it was there wouldn't of been no trough inside, only a natural water hole. A trough would keep wild ones away for a long time and would scare them to finally leave for some other watering place. This corral, as the kids figured, was mostly for half wild stock that was hard to run in.

There was two gates to the corral, but the second gate wasn't rigged so it could be swung closed from a distance like the first. Then as the kids got up to get a few more sips of the good water and looked thru the bars of that gate they seen that it opened into a pasture. They hadn't noticed the fence before. So, as they figured it, whatever stock was caught in the corral could be turned into the pasture and held there. They noticed that the spring which furnished water for the corral opened in the pasture, and the stock put in there wouldn't have to come into the corral to water, so the corral could be left open all the time, ready for whatever stock might come in.

The kids figured that the trap corral they now was in would sure come in handy if their horses ever come to it to water. But thinking that their horses had gone on past when they lost their tracks they hardly expected 'em to ever come to that corral. If they had been shod the kids could of told their tracks apart from them of other horses which had come up the trail into the corral and then they'd seen where their horses had come in to water there that day, but their horses was unshod and their tracks was pretty well the same of any of the others.

Anyway, the kids thought, being they was there they'd just as well investigate as to how that corral gate closed and where from if they'd ever want to use the corral, and if not to catch their own horses they'd maybe catch some others that would do. It was no country to be afoot in.

They took a few more sips of water. They now felt a little water logged but they was still thirsty, and now that was relieved some their hunger begin to come back on 'em. So, being that the prospects wasn't good there they put their minds to getting some way of getting somewhere somehow and of getting something to eat in as short a time as possible. That way would come with catching themselves some horses they could ride, and the trap corral might come in handy that way.

From the corral they couldn't see where the wire led to thru the grove of quakers. They climbed over, and following the wire that was stretched up above 'em they went thru a small patch of willows that was around the spring, and then, as they looked ahead thru the grove of quakers they received, as they figured at the time, the biggest and most pleasant surprise of their lives, for about fifty yards from them was a low, dirt-roofed log cabin.

It was hard to see at first on account it blended so well with the lights and shadows of the quakers, and they hardly believed their eyes when they made it out. But there it was, sure enough, and the sight of it more than cheered their hearts, for a cabin to them meant people and food, and that goes mighty well with a person that's lost and hungry.

The kids forgot about following the wire as they found the plain trail that led from the corral to the cabin. They

About fifty yards away was a low, dirt-roofed log cabin.

rushed up to it, holding down cheering hollers, and on to the stone slabs that made a little porch to the front of the cabin. The door was closed, and they wondered a little. Then Kip knocked. There was no answer. He looked at Scootie as he waited a while and then feeling sure nobody was inside he pulled the latch string and opened the door.

The two small windows lighted the inside of the cabin well and the kids went on in. After the first glance around, Scootie noticed that there was no curtains on the windows and figured right away that no lady had been around. But the place had been lived in, and seemed like not any longer ago than the night before. Kip felt of the small iron stove, it was still warm. Then, looking around a bit, he spied a pot on a low shelf in a corner. He walked over to it, and raising the lid he looked down into the finest looking mixture of cooked food he thought he'd ever seen. He hollered at Scootie who was also investigating around, found a spoon to stir into the mixture, and as the two looked and sniffed at it they sudden lost interest for all else around 'em.

The kids had bumped into a heap better luck than they could ever hoped. They didn't realize that right then, they was too hungry, but they more than appreciated it. The mixture in the pot was made up into a stew of tomatoes, macaroni, pieces of salt pork, and as the kids stirred the stew up some more they seen hunks of dark meat with fine bones. It was sage chicken.

There was kindling and wood by the stove, and Kip wasn't long in starting a fire and putting the stew on to warm up.

Scootie went to investigating around the shelves above where the stew pot had been located and found a can with a few baking powder biscuits in it. They sure would go well, cold or hot. She hunted for butter but found none. The sugar was on a table by a window and in a big baking powder can with the lid on to keep the flies off. The salt and pepper was beside it, also in baking powder cans but smaller and with holes punched in the lids.

Some plates and knives and forks was brought down out of the shelves and the table was soon set. The kids didn't bother about making tea or coffee for the stew and biscuits would sure do, with some more good water to drink.

In a short while they was sitting at the table, the stew pot with a big spoon in it holding the center on an old magazine for a pad, and the kids went at it from there. Sure a dream, they thought, in comparison to how they felt only an hour or so before. There was sure no promise of food or water then and they had no idea as to when they would get any for a long time to come.

They was apt to gulp down their food as they started to eat, but after the first few mouthfuls, and thinking of how they'd done with the water they looked at one another with warnings once again and slowed down to tasting what they et. It all tasted mighty good, far better it seemed, than anything they'd ever et before and there was no easing their appetites for quite a spell. But finally, and as they got more satisfied, they got to thinking that they'd better quit before they made themselves sick. They could eat more later and it would be well if they saved some for then, and they also thought of whoever lived there, when he came in.

They finished up on biscuits and lick (syrup) and called it all a mighty fine meal. Scootie had put some water on the stove and while she washed the dishes and put things back in place, Kip went out and cut some wood and kindling to replace what he'd used, all of which was from the teachings Uncle Bill had given them as to the rules of the range country. To leave things as they'd been found.

After all was in order again in the cabin the kids took on a very much needed rest. Scootie stretched out on the one bunk where there was some soogans (quilts) and blankets covered over with a tarpaulin. It wasn't a soft bed, it would of been better layed on the ground, but it was very restful.

Kip went outside and stretched out on the ground and soon, him and Scootie was sound asleep, wore out from travel and the suffering of thirst and hunger which now was eased. They'd thought no more as to about where they was, their horses, or how they was going to get back to the ranch. That could be attended to later.

They might of slept on till dark and on thru the night, but as the hot sun got close to setting and the shadows crept up on the quaker grove, Kip begin to stir and curl up some, he was getting to feel a little cold. That kind of half woke him up, and then some sounds thru the earth done the rest. He sat up and listened, the sounds came from the corral, and squinting thru the quakers and where the willows wasn't so thick he could see the legs of some stock there and watering at the trough. He jumped up at the sight and with only one thought in mind, to pull on the wire and close the gate on whatever stock was in the corral. He didn't waste time to see if the stock was cattle or horses or if it might be their two horses or any they could use. If they wasn't anything he would want he could always turn 'em loose again. He made the two steps to the corner of the cabin in one jump, for there's where he'd noticed the wire to the corral gate was fastened. He pulled on the wire with all his strength and weight, it pulled easy enough and in a split second he heard the gate slam and the catch fall in place to hold it.

There was a scrambling noise as the gate slammed shut, and Kip figured from the sound of it that whatever he'd caught sure wasn't of the gentle kind. He hollered at Scootie but she didn't come to life until he told her he'd caught something in the corral. She jumped up at that, and rubbing her eyes followed him to the corral.

What they found there was three horses, pretty wild ones, and they snorted and crowded the far side of the corral. They was good looking horses, and fat as seals. Two of them had very plain saddle marks on their backs, which went to show that they'd rode aplenty. Kip and Scootie figured they might try 'em, thinking they might do to get back to the ranch on, but they was mighty dubious as to being able to catch 'em, even in the corral, let alone riding 'em, for them horses sure did act spooky and not at all of the kind that could be rode bareback and with only a rope around their nose.

They didn't feel like trying 'em that evening anyhow, but they decided to keep them and turn them in the pasture adjoining the corral, then they figured they would run them in afoot the next morning and try 'em. They would be pretty well rested up by then and they would have their strength back again. They thought they would need all of that to handle them horses.

Before turning the horses in the pasture they read the brands on 'em, they was easy brands to read but they'd never seen or heard of 'em before, and being that one of the horses, the one without the saddle marks, packed the Five Barb brand on him they figured the other two also belonged to their Uncle Frank, for he owned many horses bearing different brands.

They opened the corral gate to the pasture and the horses went out of the corral a snorting and as tho they'd been shot out of a cannon.

"They're sure wild," says Kip.

"Yes," Scootie agreed, "and I think we'll have a hard time corralling them again, afoot like we are."

Then it came to them as they watched the horses run for the high places in the pasture, that they didn't know how big the pasture was and if it was up and in shape all around to hold 'em. The sun was just going down over a far western ridge but it would still be light for near an hour, and the kids figured they'd better go around the fence before dark, if they could. They opened the trap gate of the corral as it was before, then closed the other gate to the pasture and the corral was again ready for any other stock that might come in.

In a box by the cabin they found a pair of plyers, a hammer and some staples and with that they figured they could repair the fence if need be. They started from the corral, and from there it looked like it was up and in good shape, plenty high and tight and made to hold horses. As they went on they was satisfied that it had been well kept up right along and they didn't think there'd be much use of going around it, but they wanted to make sure and, besides, they wanted to find out how big the pasture was.

They didn't have to go so far before they seen it wasn't so very big, and they was glad for that when they thought of having to wrangle the horses afoot. But even tho the pasture wasn't very big the grass growed mighty well there, it was tall and thick and could easy take care of thirty head of horses the year around if needed to.

The kids seen the three horses they'd turned out of the corral, they was running along the fence on the other side of the pasture and seeing for themselves if there was a hole in it. Then they seen other horses, eight more, but them wasn't running. They was just grazing quiet and like they was very much at home in the pasture, and the kids, wanting to find out what horses they was, went to look 'em over. The horses let 'em come close enough so their brands could be read, but that gave no information, for they'd never before seen or heard of the brands the horses was packing, and they'd never seen the horses before either. But they seemed gentle and maybe they'd do to borrow if the three they'd trapped proved too wild. It would be a case of necessity if they did.

It was getting dark, and the kids hurried on to look the rest of the fence over while they could see. Soon enough they was getting near the corral again. The fence was in good condition, and they'd only had to put in a couple of staples. They was going along the fence and getting close to the corral when Kip stopped short in his tracks and held out a hand for Scootie to do the same and be quiet. For coming up the trail to the corral he seen the dark shapes of what looked to be two horses. Being still hopeful of catching their own horses, and making sure that the two dark shapes was horses, and maybe their own, Kip whispered to Scootie to stay where she was and he would go to the cabin and pull the gate closed on 'em after they got into the corral, that would be the best and surest way. He was careful not to make any noise as he went for fear of scaring the horses back, and as he soon reached the cabin he waited a while to give the horses time to get in the corral and to the trough.

He hadn't noticed it before, but while he waited at the cabin and where the wire was fastened he found out that there was a little opening thru the quaker grove and willows, and from where he was, even while near dark, he could see pretty well into the corral and any stock that might be in there. He realized too that the cabin couldn't be seen from the corral, only the place where he was standing, but

He seen the horses come into the corral and head for the trough.

a feller would have to look close from there, and could see only thru the opening.

He seen the horses come into the corral and head for the trough, and as they started to drink he pulled on the wire and closed the gate on 'em. There wasn't as much commotion as there had been when the first three horses had been caught, and from that Kip figured them two was of a gentler kind. When he got to the corral, Scootie was already there and as the two got together and closer to the horses they soon recognized 'em, and they come near hugging one another at the sight of 'em. For the two horses was none other than their own two good and gentle ones.

CHAPTER EIGHT

KIP'S AND SCOOTIE'S HORSES had felt their thirst too and had come to water there for the second time that day. It was with a great relief and happy feeling that the kids got their own horses again. Now they could go and get their saddles and try to find their way back to the ranch, and they'd be careful not get set afoot again. If they wandered and got lost more they would try and find water and good grass for their horses before hobbling 'em out for the night. . . . They'd look around the cabin before leaving for something to make better hobbles with than the hard twist ropes they'd used, they could maybe find some bigger and softer pieces of rope, a couple of gunny sacks, twisted up, would do fine.

They let the horses drink all they wanted and then walked up to 'em, that was easy enough to do while they was in the corral. Scootie reached down and felt below her horse's ankles, the hair was only ruffled a little but not rubbed off. Kip also reached to feel of his horse's ankles and the hair was more than ruffled on his, it was rubbed off down to the hide. It was sore like a burn, and when he touched the places the horse flinched.

"Well," he says, "I guess mine was the second one to lose his hobbles."

He went to the cabin and got some mixed grease he'd
found in a lard bucket there and rubbed plenty of that on
the rope-burned places. Axle grease or heated tallow would
of been better but there wasn't none of that there. Anyhow
the horse wasn't burnt bad, it wouldn't bother him to travel,
and when the doctoring was done and the horses didn't
seem to want any more water, Kip opened the corral gate
to the pasture and started 'em out, loose. They'd be safe
in there and on good feed, and the kids knew they could
be corralled easy enough afoot.

It was good and dark by the time they got back to the
cabin, and the kids begin to look for matches to light the
lamp with. Kip had found some to light the fire with that
afternoon, and now that it was dark and he needed some

And rubbed plenty of that on the rope-burned places.

more he remembered well how he'd liked to've had some of them matches while on the long ridge the night before. He found the matches and lit one, Scootie found the lamp, and soon there was a good light in the cabin. . . . And before he would forget, Kip took some of the matches. He also reminded Scootie of the evening before and advised her to take some too.

"We both have pockets in our shirts," he told her, "and you can't tell when sometime one of us might run out of matches, and when we might need 'em the most."

Scootie agreed with him, and remarked as she took some of the matches that they was the queerest she'd ever seen. They was the chinese block matches, the sulphur kind where one is pulled off as needed and lit on the same block, and as is said about 'em on the range, "the kind you never run out of."

The lighted lamp made things mighty homey and cheerful-like in the cabin. Sure some contrast from the night before, the kids thought. Now, as they sat on the bunk and looked around, their appetites went to calling again. Kip went and got a fresh bucket of water at the spring, they drank some and then Scootie filled a kettle to put on the stove while Kip started the fire, they'd have tea or coffee with their meal that evening.

The evening was cool again and a fire went well, and as the wood crackled in the stove, the kids went to thinking about what they would have for the next meal. They didn't want to eat up the rest of the stew, as much as they'd liked to, because they figured that whoever had cooked it might be back most any time, and most likely very hungry.

They begin looking around to see what else they could find to make a fair meal out of. In sacks and boxes under the pot shelf was quite a few things, all that was necessary for the good of an empty stomach, but there was no fresh meat, nor ham, nor bacon, only sow belly (salt pork). Then there was no eggs nor no butter nor no milk, and that sort of put the kids up a stump as to what to cook.

While on trips with Uncle Bill, in the mountains and other places, they took pack horses loaded with camp outfit and grub along. They'd watched the old cowboy and even helped some while he'd cook a meal, very good and appetizing meals, and from only very plain things. There was nothing fancy like butter or eggs or jams ever brought along, and still, Uncle Bill could make fancy enough and good tasting spreads out of only the very necessary. Flour and rice, raisins and bacon, and baking powder and salt was his main stem, and he could mix them things around in different ways so as to make a two course meal that'd sure be easy to take, stick to the ribs and wouldn't leave no bad taste in a feller's gizard.

Sugar and coffee was as something extra, and if small game could be got while along the trail to sort of add on with the main things why that all would be the makings of a very luxurious meal.

It had seemed so easy for Uncle Bill to think up and cook so many things out of so little to choose from and, as the kids watched him, they figured it *was* easy. But now that the old cowboy wasn't around it seemed like their imagination was blank or stayed back with him, and it wasn't at all easy to think up something to cook that would appeal to them. It wasn't that they was hard to please or wasn't hungry enough, but they wanted to cook something that would look and taste like it was fit to eat and satisfy the stomach.

As they looked the grub supply over and over they seen that it was mighty plain but there was a good variety and a lot more things than Uncle Bill ever took on any trip. They thought of him, and they knowed that he sure could of figured up something good to cook and right quick out of the pile of grub they was staring at.

They could of cooked some beans or some such like things which would be good, they thought, but that would take a half a day or so. They wanted to think up of something that would cook up in about an hour and no longer, for their appetites was good again. As they stared at the different things they'd sorted out they went to thinking of what all they'd watched Uncle Bill cook and which had tasted so good, they named quite a few things to each other, and then finally decided on three or four which they thought they could cook and go well together to make up a meal.

They started with the rice, figuring on boiling enough of that to do for the main part of the meal and also for the dessert. For the main part of the meal the grease from fried salt pork would be spread over the rice, the salt pork could be et with it too. Then for the dessert some raisins could be cooked up with part of the rice and maybe a little sugar added. To go with that, Kip figured on making bannocks. There's different ways of making that, some very flat and stiff but tasty, and Kip thought of adding on a little baking powder to make it lighter, then with a pinch of salt in the flour he made a stiff dough from which he cut out pieces and flattened in a hot pan with the back of his hand as he'd seen Uncle Bill do. The bannocks Uncle Bill had made had tasted mighty good.

With that they decided to open a can of tomatoes to stew, and with coffee, they couldn't find no tea, they figured that would make a meal that wouldn't be so hard to take, not if it was cooked right.

They, of course, done their best to cook the meal right. They tried to remember how Uncle Bill had cooked just such as they was cooking, and they remembered pretty well, but they soon found out that watching a thing being done is a lot easier than doing it yourself. Like with the rice, they put too much of it in the pot and when it swelled they had two potsful. Then they didn't parboil the salt pork before frying and they fried most of the grease out of it so that when they got thru they had not much left but shrunk, brittle and salty pieces, but the raisins for the rice pudding turned out all right, so did the stewed tomatoes and coffee, and as for the bannocks, Scootie grinned and remarked that they'd take the places of dog biscuits, if a dog was hungry enough.

But all in all they sort of enjoyed the meal, and their appetites was satisfied. They dirdied a lot of tin dishes and pots but they'd had some fun in mixing things and cooking 'em. And when they got thru and got up from the table they didn't stop to rest much but went right to work at cleaning up the pots and pans and everything they'd used, for they expected that at any time whoever lived in the cabin might be coming in, and they didn't want anybody to see the mess they'd made.

It didn't take 'em long to clean things up again and put all to order as it had been, and it wasn't long after that when, as they sat down to rest that they begin to get sleepy. They was still tired, and even tho the rest they'd had that afternoon more than helped 'em they felt like they could sure take on some more. They would of proceeded to do that but they sort of expected the man who lived there back any time and they didn't want to be caught asleep when he came in. They knowed that there sure wasn't no certain hours for a rider, and one might as likely come in in the middle of the night as in the middle of the day, and being that it hadn't been dark over a couple of hours, the kids thought it best to stay up a while longer before stretching out for their needed rest.

Scootie wasn't as sleepy as Kip was, for she was a little leary of what whoever lived in the cabin might be like, and as she said to Kip once, he might be a rustler or horsethief or some kind of an outlaw, the way the cabin was so well hid. Kip sort of laughed at that, saying that the cabin was hid so as not to scare what spooky stock came to water at the corral, that no such outlaw would live in any certain place like where they was and wouldn't go to the bother or have the time to build a cabin. And even if it was an outlaw that lived in it, he'd most likely be mighty decent to meet, for as Uncle Bill had said the range outlaw looks and acts the least like one and is more apt to help a person in trouble than anybody else because he's most always in trouble himself and knows what that is.

But Kip's talk didn't go much towards quieting Scootie's uneasy feelings, and about the only way it helped was that it made a noise.

The range outlaw looks and acts the least like one.

Kip got up from the rawhide covered chair he'd been sitting on, yawned and stretched, and to keep himself awake begin looking around the cabin. He'd looked around before but he'd been so busy, either with helping with the meals or cleaning up afterwards, that he hadn't had the chance to take a good look.

The inside walls of the log cabin had been hewed flat, and covering the most of it, like a wall paper, was pictures and drawings cut out of papers and magazines and pasted with syrup or a paste of flour and water or whatever might of been handy at the time. In some places the pictures was pasted over one another and made a layer of three or four thick. The run of 'em was about everything in general, from magazine cover girls to battleships and from insects to mountain peaks, even to pieces of poetry and songs. There was pictures and cartoons of the west, south, north and east, some tragic, some quiet and peaceful and others comical, and the first ones that'd been pasted on the walls dated back some forty years, which, Kip figured, was about the time when the cabin was built.

The pictures made an interesting wall paper, and Kip kept well awake looking at 'em. He talked to Scootie about different pictures and then she also got interested to looking at 'em, so well that she forgot her uneasiness some.

"Gee," says Kip as he was about thru looking at the pictures, "I'd sure like to have a cabin so I could fix it up like this."

He looked the inside of the cabin over good so if he ever got one he'd fix it just like it, even to the stove and table. The table, like the door and window casings, was of planed lumber and had been made right there. There was many brands cut and burned on the door, and amongst 'em the kids recognized their Uncle Frank's main brands. There wasn't many of the others that they could read. Above the door was a repeating rifle on two wooden pegs. At the sight of it, Scootie felt all the more that the man living there was an outlaw, but Kip said no to that, that if the man was an outlaw he'd of took the rifle with him.

By the side of the door was a bench the water bucket was on, a dipper hanging above it. On the same bench was a wash basin and a bar of soap in the lid of a can. A towel, not so dirty, hung above the basin and underneath a little shelf where there was a looking glass, not cracked, and a straight razor and cup for a shaving mug, and then a comb. Beside the bench was a three shelf stand made of more planed lumber and which was being used for a bureau and where some few best shirts and such like was kept, the front was covered with a canvas flap. Old magazines and a writing tablet and a pencil was on the stand, also a pretty fair watch which was still running. The time showed after ten, and wether it was right or not the kids felt it was past their bed time anyhow.

The bunk, also made of planed lumber and not nailed to the wall, was on the opposite corner from the stand. On the corner opposite the bunk was the stove, and between it and the other corner where the grub and dishes was stacked and shelved was the table. A good wood box was back of the stove and beside it and against the wall was a piece of canvas, tacked and against which a couple of frying pans and a griddle hung.

Everything was handy and fitting to the comfort of a range man, and like most such places it was clean, there was no unnecessary curtains to keep the light coming in from the windows, and no paint to color up the wood work, the sun and light done its own coloring and made it all mellow. The ceiling of planed lumber above the heavy ridge logs had turned to a deep, rich red cedar color from the many years of cooking smoke that had soared up there during meal time of winters. The floor of foot-wide boards was darker than pine wood color and there was a few stains on it. The knots didn't wear down like the softer wood around 'em did and they stuck up like well polished carbuncles here and there. It was cleaned often enough by throwing a couple of soapy bucketfuls of water over it and scrubbing with a broom, then more bucketfuls for the final cleaning.

The cabin was about twenty feet wide by twenty-five feet long, the logs of the walls was thick, averaging about fourteen inches thru and rested on a rough foundation of stone, just high enough so's to keep the bottom log off the ground. For the roof there was foot-wide boards layed over five heavy ridge logs, two layers of tar paper over the boards, and then about five inches of shaly dirt spread over the whole thing. It made a heavy roof but, like the rest of the house, it sure held out the cold, and it was cool inside during the hottest of summer days.

It was such a cabin as can be seen in most parts of the range country and used as cow camps, or by sourdoughs (bachelors) on their own little spread. Of course there's some not as well built as that one was or of as heavy logs, that all depends on what can be got to build with and they're not called cabins but either camps or houses. The one just described would be called either a camp or a house but Kip and Scootie called it a cabin, and most likely only because it was made of logs. Anyway they liked it a lot more than they would of a mansion. Specially Kip, and Scootie would of also liked it as much if it hadn't been for the uneasy way she felt about who might be living there and maybe coming in during the night. If it had been daytime she wouldn't of minded so much.

Being tired she begin to get drowsy, and sleep would of relieved her, but she didn't feel so safe in going to sleep right yet and she forced herself to keep awake. Looking around for something to keep her interested she seen a pair of silver mounted spurs hanging on a peg with a rope and by some clothes. She took 'em down to look at 'em, they was good spurs, and valuable, and as she fingered 'em she remarked, more like to make talk, that she thought the man who lived there would be afraid to leave these spurs with the cabin unlocked, then she mentioned the rifle, the watch on the stand and other things that could easy be stolen and carried away on a horse.

Kip was about to go to sleep standing up himself but he woke up pretty well at Scootie's talk. He of a sudden remembered of Uncle Bill talking to them on the subject which she'd now brought up, and he proceeded to freshen her memory as to it. He reminded her of how Uncle Bill had said that locks hadn't been known in the range country until the homesteaders drifted in thick in some parts and brought other kinds of people with 'em who didn't trust nobody and who nobody trusted. So padlocks begin to come into use, but before that was done, Uncle Bill had said, there was a few thieves here and there got caught with what they'd stole from ranches and camps before they could get very far and then got no further than the closest tree, where they was hung. For raiding ranches or camps while the owner was gone was considered to be about the meanest kind of crime, so low that in comparison horse stealing would be an honor, and men was hung for that too.

A petty thief is more than hated in the range country, and on account of such kind and their doings the range folks had to lock up when going away for a few days. One such a thief would affect a whole territory that way, and that's why that when one was caught before he got to the shelter of towns and laws, which often happened, things went mighty hard with him, even if he only stole a pair of spurs.

Locks are now in use in some parts of the range country and where automobiles travel thru, but far inland from graveled roads and where trails are still for horses and cattle

When a rider comes to some shelter, maybe tired and cold and hungry.

the ranch houses and camps are without locks when the owner goes away, even if for a month or more. That's the old custom and according with the hospitality of the range country so that when a rider comes to some shelter, maybe tired and cold and hungry he can come inside, make use of the kindling that's always on hand, warm up and cook himself something to eat. He can take care of his horse the same way and help himself to hay and grain for him. There's no return asked or wanted for that hospitality, only that the kindling and wood is replaced and everything cleaned and left as it was found so that if the owner or some other cold and hungry rider came along afterwards he could easy make himself to home.

Taking advantage of that hospitality is considered pretty bad and whoever does is thought of as worse than a bum. The range country has no use for bums.

Kip memorized on the subject and talked on it pretty well. He talked as well to freshen his own memory on it as he did Scootie's, besides it kept him awake. He went on talking while still looking at the pictures on the walls, and he'd went on some more, but glancing to the bunk and where Scootie had been sitting he seen that he was without a listener, for she was curled up there and sound asleep.

He grinned a little and then he spoke to her. "Well," he says, "I think we can at least pull our boots off for tonight."

The change in Kip's tone of voice half woke Scootie up, and as she heard him throw one of his boots on the floor she sat up, very sleepy-eyed.

"Yes," Kip repeated, "I think we'd better pull our boots off for tonight, and if you'll give me a little room I'll sleep on the bunk too. I don't think we'll need any covers."

Scootie only about half heard him, and she didn't have a word to say as she pulled her boots off, and then leaving room for Kip she curled up again. Kip stretched out on his side of the bunk and in half a minute the two was sound asleep, as sound, and maybe sounder as if they'd been in their own soft and cozy beds at their home in the far away big city.

That's the way Uncle Bill found 'em when less than an hour later he walked into the cabin and lit a match to see.

CHAPTER NINE

THE SUN WAS AN HOUR HIGH and the meadow larks was singing their best when Kip's eyes begin to blink and then open. He wondered where he was for a while, it being morning and him with his clothes all on but his boots, but as he looked around at the walls of the cabin and seen the sun shine on the quakers thru the window he soon figured out his whereabouts and how he come there. He glanced over at Scootie who was still curled up about the same as the night before and then he thought a while as to what the new day might bring and if him and Scootie would find their way back to the ranch before that night. But laying and thinking don't get a feller nowheres much, besides he was hungry, and breakfast had better be thought of first.

He got up, stretched and went to put on his boots, and as he started building a fire and walking around the cabin his bootheels made just enough noise on the bare wood floor to wake Scootie up. She too wondered where she was, but as she heard the sharp sounds of Kip's bootheels and the crackling of the wood in the stove she also soon realized. She didn't have much time to lay and think, for soon as Kip seen her move he, in a good natured

Out a little ways was a man standing over a coffee pot by a fire.

way, told her to get up and make a hand of herself, that there was a big day ahead.

Kip opened the door to go out and get a bucket of water, then, what he seen as he did near made him drop his bucket in surprise, for out a little ways was a man standing over a coffee pot by a fire, and the man was Uncle Bill. . . . He let out a holler at the sight of him and run over to him, and Scootie, still by the bunk, run to the door with only one boot on, wondering.

"You lazy wollopers," says the old cowboy, looking at Kip after he'd got near and then at the running and laughing Scootie. "I thought you'd never get up. Here I've got breakfast all ready and I was afraid I'd have to eat it all by myself."

But Kip and Scootie wasn't much worried about breakfast right then, for there couldn't be no thought for food with their surprise at the presence of the old cowboy. They went to jabbering like they hadn't seen him for months instead of only two nights and a day, but they'd missed and needed him more during the last two nights and one day than any month any other time.

The old cowboy grinned at their so happy and wide awake faces, with the look of sleep that was still on 'em, and finally telling 'em to wash up he went on to the cabin to get the necessary dishes to eat out of, for, as he'd said, an outside-cooked meal should be et outside.

The night before, and while the kids was asleep, he'd tiptoed in the cabin in his stocking feet and got what he'd needed to cook himself something to eat with, outside and where he slept, also enough to do for breakfast. Seeing that the kids had been resting so well that night he hadn't wanted to wake 'em up, for he'd figured they sure needed it.

The breakfast of flapjacks and salt pork, fried potatoes and onion, syrup made of sugar and water, and strong coffee went well all around, and as the three squatted on the ground with their plates resting between their knees there was many words went with the many mouthfuls. Nothing was said about the meal, nor even the salt pork tasting good, for Uncle Bill had cooked it and that was enough said right there.

What was the most on the kids' minds right then was how Uncle Bill found 'em, and so soon, and between mouthfuls, Scootie asked him.

"That was easy enough," answered the old cowboy. "When I got to the ranch with the horses and seen that you kids wasn't there as I expected, nor even seen any sign of yuz on the big flat from the horse range, I figured something had went wrong with you two (to save their feelings he didn't say he was sure they'd got lost), so I saddled up a fresh horse, figured abouts where I'd find you, and here I am. I got here last night and you two was asleep so I didn't bother you. I'd of got here sooner, maybe by noon yesterday but my horse got one front foot wedged in between two dead timbers in the hills and sprained his ankle. He got pretty lame and I had to walk and lead him about halfways from there to here."

Scootie came pretty near saying that it was odd that all three came to the camp afoot, even Uncle Bill, but she thought better of it, for it seemed like the old cowboy didn't know that her and Kip had also walked in, and she didn't care to tell him, figuring that being lost was bad enough. Kip also thought of the same thing and also kept quiet, but as they looked at one another, understanding, they wondered. They wondered if he'd followed their trail. If he had he'd know for sure they'd lost their horses, for their boot prints had been right over the horses' tracks, and thinking of the day before, if Uncle Bill could of got to the camp by noon and he'd been on their trail he'd of caught up with 'em about the middle of the forenoon and not so far from where they'd left their saddles. But that would only made things worse, they thought, because Uncle Bill would only had to ride on to find their horses, and about all they could of done would of been to wait, or walk some to meet him coming back, and feeling sheepish all the while.

Now they felt as tho they hadn't put the old cowboy to so very much trouble. They'd got their horses themselves, and now that they was well rested and their thirst and hunger all satisfied, they felt like they'd be good for a long time again, but they'd sure made up their minds that, if possible, they'd never be left behind as Uncle Bill had left 'em while running the horses. They'd sure do their best to follow him, for they somehow felt mighty helpless and lost while away from him, and the country looked so much bigger and mysterious and desolate.

"Well," says the old cowboy, after the dishes was all washed and put back in the cabin and all things replaced there as they'd been found, "do you youngsters feel like you can stand the ride back to the ranch today? . . . I think Martha will be some worried about yuz."

"Yes, I think we can make it," says Scootie, "if you don't start running after another bunch of wild horses on the way."

Uncle Bill grinned, then got serious. "That reminds me," he says, "I'm afoot. . . . My horse will be too lame to move this morning, and if old Zeb hasn't got any horses here I can ride why I guess I'll have to hoof it."

That got the kids to thinking. There was the three horses they'd caught before they'd got their own two, and maybe one of them three would do. And when Uncle Bill was told about 'em he remarked that he'd try most anything before walking.

"Let's wrangle 'em in," he says.

As they started out to get the horses, Scootie, who was still wondering about who lived in the cabin, asked about old Zeb which Uncle Bill had mentioned and if he was the man who lived there.

"Yes," says Uncle Bill. "This is one of your Uncle Frank's camps, and old Zeb is watching over a bunch of thorough-bred cattle your uncle runs up higher here during summer. It's the herd he raises his pure-bred bulls from and he keeps a man watching over 'em all the time so that no other cattle stray in among 'em or that none of 'em get away. They're valuable cattle and they're kept in a big pasture. Old Zeb is an old has-been like myself and likes to hibernate like this, but he hasn't come to his senses yet so far as riding is concerned and he still has an idea that he can ride the rough ones. Consequences is he hasn't got a horse in his string I'd give a whoop for."

"But I didn't see Uncle Frank's brand on any of the horses he has in this pasture," says Kip. "Are they his own?"

"Yes, they are. He has a strong weakness for horse trading, and being he couldn't do that with the outfit's horses he keeps and rides his own. He tries to make a trade with every rider that comes along, sometimes he'll go a long ways to make up one with neighboring stockmen and he'll trade for most any kind of horse or horses so long as he sees he'll win some by it. He has made some very good trades, and once in a while he'll have fifteen to twenty horses in his string, then he'll turn around and maybe trade three or four for one perticular horse that gets his eye. Horse trading is his big enjoyment. He'd rather do that than eat even if he was starving, and most of his horses are only trading stock, meaning that they might be good or stove up some-how, or else spoiled and worthless as for any range work, the kind that's apt to go to bucking or stampeding in scary places or when there's work to be done."

As Uncle Bill talked, Scootie seen how useless her fears had been. Of course Uncle Bill didn't tell of what he knowed of old Zeb's past as a mighty reckless horse thief, cattle rustler and all around gun-toting range outlaw. But if the kids had met him they'd only found him very good and cheerful company. He could of told 'em many stories which would of made 'em laugh till tears come to their eyes, and others that would of brought lumps in their throats. Scootie now wished that old Zeb had rode in on 'em and, of course, Kip also wished the same. They might come to the cabin again some day they thought, without being lost, and get to visit with him.

In a short while, Uncle Bill seen old Zeb's eight horses, then the kid's two, and as he looked around from a high point in the pasture, wondering where the three horses the kids had said they'd caught he finally spotted 'em, sort of hiding and sunning themselves behind a high rocky ledge. Being that the kids' horses had been located he was now more than interested in seeing what them three horses was, for out of them he hoped to pick out one he could ride back to the ranch on. He didn't want to take one of old Zeb's horses if he could help it.

Uncle Bill told the kids to come along behind him, and then he took the lead to get above the three horses by the rocky ledge. Wild horses will sometimes sense a human without scent or sight of him, and the three horses behind the ledge acted as tho they had, for as Uncle Bill and the kids walked to get above them the horses came up to the point of the rocky ledge and looked around like to investigate.

The old cowboy, mighty surprised, squatted in his tracks behind a brush and motioned for the kids to do the same. He could hardly believe his eyes as he looked at the three horses, for they was the three renegades that had given him so much trouble only a couple of days before and which he'd made up his mind to get, regardless of how much hard riding he'd have to do. And here they was. The kids had got 'em for him.

The kids hadn't been close enough to the three horses while Uncle Bill was running them so they could recognize 'em when they caught 'em, and they was also surprised and pleased that them three they'd caught was the same renegades. And, as the old cowboy told them, they sure had saved him or other riders plenty of hard riding, which would of had to've been done to get 'em.

They was the three renegades.

But as the old cowboy looked at the three spooky acting horses he wondered if they *was* caught, for even tho they was in a pasture and close to a corral he had a hunch that a wire fence wouldn't hold 'em any more than it would a deer if a rider crowded 'em a little too much. They would skip over or thru it, and then it would be impossible to corral 'em. Uncle Bill would hardly count them three horses as caught until they was in corral strong and high enough to hold them, and then they wouldn't safely be rid of until they was shipped to some farming country a thousand miles or more away and where they couldn't get back from. They would lose a lot of their wildness when shipped that way, and being worked and in strange country where there's no range land they would soon gentle and resign themselves to staying in one small place.

That's what Uncle Bill figured on doing with 'em, shipping 'em out of the country before they spoiled more bunches of behaving range horses to running against a rider and that's what Uncle Bill decided would be the first thing to do.

But getting the three renegades into the corral would be the ticklish job, after that he'd make sure they wouldn't get away again. He explained his plan to Kip and Scootie of how he was going to try and corral the horses. He knowed they sure couldn't be corralled afoot, and that's what Uncle Bill decided would be the first thing to do.

Keeping out of sight from the renegades they went to get the two horses, and them two didn't cause any trouble, they went right into the corral. Uncle Bill caught and saddled one of 'em, it was Kip's, then to make double sure the trap gate leading in from the outside would stay closed he wired it tight in a couple of places. He then opened wide the gate that led in from the pasture, and left Scootie's horse free to go back in the pasture and join his lame horse which was grazing in the tall grass near the spring. The sight of them two would sort of help to quiet the renegades as they would be brought near the corral.

He'd already told the kids that the best way they could help him would be for them to keep as much out of sight and quiet as possible, for, as he'd explained to them, one rider could do as well as four in getting the renegades in the corral from the small pasture, it would be less to spook 'em and maybe cause 'em to hit thru the fence. Then again, the kids not being at all experienced to the ticklish work could only cause trouble by showing up at the wrong place and at the wrong time. So he'd told them to get up along on the outside of the fence if they wanted to and to where they could hide and watch.

The kids hit for a good high hiding place quite a ways from the corral and Uncle Bill started out after the ren-egades. First he stirred up old Zeb's string of horses and spooked 'em so they would run some when he brought the three renegades to mix in with 'em. If they stood still the renegades would go right on by 'em, but if they run a little they'd be more apt to stay with 'em and maybe all the way on into the corral. The old cowboy figured strong on Zeb's horses checking up the renegades in the wild runs he knowed they would make.

After he'd started Zeb's horses he left 'em trotting along the fence and heading towards the corral. If he could only get the renegades to run along the same way now and catch up with 'em before they got to the corral all might be good. But as he got sight of the renegades and they seen him at about the same time they sort of blowed up and went plumb wild. Uncle Bill stopped his horse for fear that even at the distance he was from them they would run thru the fence. He seen at a glance that it wouldn't do to try to run or crowd 'em for a while, not if he wanted to keep them inside the pasture. He just sat his horse in plain sight and let 'em run. It was better for him to stay in plain sight that way because then the horses could see him and know where he was, and being wild as they was, they wouldn't be spooky of him bobbing up on 'em out of the brush and close to their heels.

The renegades run towards the fence so fast and came so close to it that for a second, Uncle Bill thought sure they'd go thru it. But quicker than a flash and when to within only a couple of inches of the wire, it seemed like, they turned and run along the fence at full speed and like the devil was after 'em.

They run the direction Zeb's horses had taken, but at the speed they was going, the old cowboy felt sure they wouldn't even slacken up when they got near them. They didn't. They run right on by 'em as tho they hadn't seen 'em, on down towards the corral. But before they got near there they left the fence and cut acrost the pasture to the other side, where they kept on running along the fence some more and back up towards the rocky ledge where Uncle Bill had first seen 'em.

There they stopped, heads and tails up and whistled their snorts. They'd run a circle of near two miles in about no time and was breathing fast. But Uncle Bill didn't give 'em much chance to take in many breaths. If they wanted to run he'd give 'em their bellyful of it and without him having to run his own horse, and being they hadn't hit the fence in their first run he felt pretty sure they wouldn't hit it in their second one.

The only difference between them renegades and the regular wild horse was that they was wise to a fence. They knowed that the wire would cut and that they'd better keep away from it if they didn't want their hides tore up, where the wild horse would never check up at a fence, for to him the little wire line looks no more dangerous than cobwebs stretching from tree to tree. The renegades was wiser than wild horses in that way and unless they was crowded or cornered or got heated up and mad they wasn't likely to hit a fence.

Uncle Bill wasn't going to crowd nor corner them, not till the right time come, and before then he'd see that they had their run pretty well out. When they got back on the rocky ledge and stopped he didn't let 'em linger there, and he didn't start after 'em like he was going to run 'em down, instead he just put his horse in a trot towards 'em, and that done the trick. The renegades snorted and started on another circle. They went past Zeb's horses in a tight run once more, cut acrost the pasture above the corral as before and to the other side. There they slowed down some, and the stretch up hill to the rocky ledge wasn't going so fast this time, but when they got up to the rocky ledge they didn't stop nor go near it but went right on and back down towards Zeb's horses again. Them horses hadn't moved much and only seemed to enjoy watching the renegades run, like Uncle Bill and the kids was doing.

As the kids squatted in their hiding places and watched the horses circle around the pasture once and then a second time they wondered why Uncle Bill didn't take after 'em and run 'em into the corral when they came toward it, the kids could see him just asitting on his horse and in plain sight. But as the horses started on their third circle of the pasture they begin to understand why, the horses wasn't running near so fast then, they'd slow down to a trot once in a while and even to a walk for a few steps. But they kept agoing according to their instinct and looking for a way out to freedom, also to ease their spooky nature.

Then the kids seen Uncle Bill beginning to ride a little, and when the renegades would begin to lag he'd ride towards 'em and they'd run on some more. The end of the third circle wound up at good speed. With the fourth circle, the old cowboy rode a little more and by the time it was over he could get pretty close to the outlaws. They wasn't tired, but getting a little winded and to where they wasn't so flighty no more. They'd had all the running they wanted, and now it was just a case of have to with 'em. Gradually, and with the fifth circle, the old cowboy begin closing in on the renegades till finally he got close enough and to where he could handle 'em without crowding too much. The horses went another spurt as he got closer but as they got going uphill and towards the rocky ledge again they slowed down and Uncle Bill had got to within a couple of hundred yards of 'em.

He left 'em to drift on then and cut acrost the pasture to stir up Zeb's horses so they'd be spooked to run when he came in sight again of the three renegades. That done he left the eight of 'em to ramble along the fence and towards the corral again, and when the renegades ambled down along the fence on the start of another circle, Uncle Bill rode in the brush and hid till they went past him towards Zeb's horses, and then he fell in behind 'em.

It was downhill going and the horses begin to running again but not with the speed of their first couple of circles, and now the old cowboy was riding, riding as the kids had seen him ride when he was chasing them same renegades in the rough country. The kids forgot about hiding in their excitement and stood up and went to jumping up and down, and it was a good thing they was away on the other side of the corral or the horses would of seen 'em and turned back.

"Gee," Kip says to Scootie, "that horse of mine can sure run, can't he?"

Zeb's horses was soon caught up with. They was trotting along a little, and as they seen the renegades coming behind them and then the rider they spurted up some, just enough so as to sort of check the renegades to mixing and running with 'em. But the sight of the rider is what had made 'em spurt, and as that rider came closer they broke into a good lope, the renegades in the lead but staying with 'em.

They was fast getting to the ticklish place, the corral, and the renegades begin to act fidgety, spooking what was ahead and the rider behind. They'd break away from the trail along the fence and back again as they got closer to the corral and they acted as tho they would break for good most any time, cut acrost the pasture as they had and hit back for the rocky ledge. Then, knowing the rider was close to them in case they made such a break, they hung back some and got to mixing with Zeb's horses more, and as all come still closer to the corral two of Zeb's horses took the lead.

The old cowboy was up in his stirrups and ready for any move the renegades might make, for from now on till the horses entered the gate of the corral was the real ticklish time. One of the renegades made a good start to break away but he'd started too quick, and being his two pardners didn't start with him, and that Uncle Bill was at exactly the right spot to head him off, he was turned back to join the bunch again.

There was still about five hundred yards to go, and the renegades was so fidgety, dodging back and forth in the bunch that Uncle Bill expected 'em to blow up any second. The quieter company of Zeb's horses was about all that held 'em, and as they got closer and closer to the corral that held 'em less and less. . . . Then, and all three at once, they did blow up, and left Zeb's horses as tho they was standing still. The leader of the three, a big roman nosed roan, hit out as tho he was bound nothing would stop him, and the other two was right close with him. . . . Uncle Bill had his horse in a tight run at the same time the renegades started. He'd been ready, and with his coiled rope in his hand, he was right at the head of 'em to turn 'em, but they wouldn't turn. He was close enough to the big roan so he could hit him on his roman nose with the coiled rope, but that didn't faze him and he kept on arunning, the others right with him and on both sides of Uncle Bill.

Thru brush and rocks, acrost washes and draws, the renegades went at top speed and Uncle Bill, riding like a wolf in the lead of 'em, was atrying hard to turn 'em. . . . It was a good thing that the renegades'd had their run or there'd been a long ride ahead and the old cowboy might have lost his lead, but as it was, and as the corral was left behind a ways they soon quieted down. Then's when Uncle Bill turned on 'em, and he fanned their tails and spooked 'em so that they was glad to hit for and mix in with Zeb's horses again, and as them horses was on the move for the corral and the two horses, Scootie's and Uncle Bill's lame one, was close by there, that all helped to lead the renegades on. The first thing they knowed they was in the corral where they snorted and turned to face the old cowboy who'd got off his panting horse to close the gate on 'em.

He was close enough to the big roan so he could hit him on his roman nose with the coiled rope.

CHAPTER TEN

UNCLE BILL felt a great relief at getting the three renegades, he'd been wanting to get them for so long. He'd come into the corral and was standing there with his rope in his hands and sizing them up along with Zeb's horses when the whole bunch rushed to one side of the corral and made it crack. The kids had come up sudden out of the brush, and hollering their surprise and pleasure, had scared the horses.

"Go easy," Uncle Bill warned without looking at 'em, "or we won't have no horses."

The kids, realizing their mistake, quieted down and looked thru the bars from outside the corral. Uncle Bill, looking the horses over, was sort of wondering what to do next. For now that he had the renegades safe, there was the question of how to keep 'em that way and get 'em to the ranch. If his horse hadn't gone lame he could of took them on in easy enough, he thought, because they'd be some tired by the time they got there and he figured they could be corralled again then without much trouble. As it was, he didn't know what kind of a horse he'd be riding and if that one could be depended on to do the work when come

138

the time. He'd be taking chances of losing them unless he was riding a good horse.

He couldn't, of course, depend on the kids to help him because they wasn't enough experienced in handling such horses as the renegades, and all he'd want of 'em would be to follow at a distance. But it wasn't decided on as yet how he would take the horses. He'd have to know more about 'em, and about the most important thing right now was to pick himself out a saddle horse.

He didn't pay much attention to Zeb's horses when it came to that because he figured that amongst such trading stock as he was always keeping he'd be apt to pick on a bum one and he wouldn't know about any one of 'em until that one was rode quite a ways. So he put his attention on the renegades. There was one amongst the three, a little bay, that caught his eye, he was spooky but he looked like a good horse and as tho he might do. The old cowboy shook a couple of coils out of his rope, made a loop and dabbed it on his head. As the loop drawed up around his neck the little bay bellered, bogged his head and made a few buck jumps, like any good horse might do after running out for a long time, but he didn't run on the rope, and after he had his little play he held his head up to face the old cowboy. He only snorted and quivered a little, and as Uncle Bill walked up to him and placed a hand on his head the little bay quieted right down and only drawed a long breath, like to say, "Time to go to work now."

If the old cowboy was surprised at the horse's sudden gentle acting the kids was a whole lot more so, for the way that horse had run with the other two, often taking the lead and seeming to be about the wisest in dodging and outrunning a rider, they figured he'd sure be a wildcat when roped. Instead he'd cooled down to behaving like any good gentle horse.

"He's sure gentle, ain't he, Uncle Bill," says Kip.

"You should say *isn't he,*" says the old cowboy, acting serious. "Ain't he ain't right, . . . and besides I haven't rode this horse yet."

He led Kip's horse inside the corral, took the saddle and bridle off of him and turned him loose amongst the others, then he proceeded to saddle the little bay. There didn't seem to be no more to saddling him than there'd been to saddling Kip's horse. He stood like he knowed very much all about it and like he'd been saddled hundreds of times. He most likely had but that doesn't mean there was no tricks to him, and the old cowboy wasn't fooled.

He winked and grinned at the kids, and says, "There's a catch in him somewheres."

There was, but not enough to disturb the old cowboy much. The little bay only crowhopped a little when Uncle Bill got on him, and when that was over and he rode him around some, the old cowboy figured that was the worst there was to him, outside of his being hard to run in and corral, which was bad.

Uncle Bill had rode his kind often, good and well behaving horses when caught and under the saddle but regular wild horses and outlaws when out on the range. But they'd quieted down soon as a rope settled around their necks, like the little bay had. He'd rode the other kind too, just the opposite, the kind that was easy to corral and acted plum gentle, till a rope touched 'em then they'd sudden change to fighting buckers, and no work could be done with 'em, for they'd wear themselves out fighting before work was started. Most of the renegades, such as Uncle Bill had in the corral, turn out to be that kind, but once in a while some good, well behaving cowhorse that's been running out a long time, will fall in with renegades, and as he follows 'em and gets onto their ways and enjoys more and more freedom he'll easy turn to be a renegade himself, as far as to being run in and corralled is concerned, but he's the good horse again once caught and topped off.

That was the kind Uncle Bill figured the little bay was, a good horse gone to the wild bunch, and now good again when under the saddle, and while sitting on him and looking at the other two horses he had a good idea as to which one was the starter of the renegade band, it was the roman-nosed, sunk-eyed big roan, one of the kind that would die fighting or kill a man before he'd pack one. He had all the earmarks of a thoroughbred outlaw, and he'd be the one that Uncle Bill would make double sure of not losing, for his kind are like a rotten apple in a barrel of good ones and needs to be got rid of. . . . The other, a sorrel horse, without the

Then they'd sudden change to fighting buckers.

saddle marks and branded, was just a young horse, wild and nervous, but the old cowboy seen no bad signs about him, and he figured that if the horse was separated from the roan, broke to ride, and then made to run with gentler ones, he would turn out to be a good horse.

The big roan was the only one of the three that didn't belong to Frank Powers, but he'd be got rid of somehow. As for the little bay, Uncle Bill now recollected how he'd heard some of the boys speak of him, and if he was half as good as he'd heard he was he'd be worth trying to keep. The same with the unbroke sorrel horse, if he turned out good.

The old cowboy felt pretty happy in having the little bay to ride. He now felt like he could handle the other two easy enough, after he'd fixed 'em the way he wanted to. He got off the little bay, led and tied him outside the corral, then, followed by the kids, he went to the cabin and started to cook a bait. It was only middle forenoon, but he was thinking of the kids, they'd et early and it would be late that day before they'd get to the ranch and eat again. He decided to warm and finish up the rest of the stew the kids had saved, there was plenty left for three and it might of spoiled before old Zeb got back. But to sort of take the place of that he started a mess of beans with plenty of salt pork throwed in, also put on some prunes to stew, then he made a batch of biscuits, enough so that when him and the kids got thru eating there would still be quite a few left. They'd be good to go with a hurry meal in case old Zeb or anybody else came in hungry. With the start the beans would have they wouldn't take long to finish cooking, and then the prunes would be done. That all would hold any man together until he could cook himself something more to his taste along with variety.

The meal was soon done and over with, the dishes washed and put away, kindling and wood replaced and all as it had been, then Uncle Bill found old Zeb's writing pad and pencil and wrote him a note. It said:

"I crippled my horse so I had to leave him here in the pasture. Use your science and doctor him up, will you. I had to borrow one of your reprobates and will bring him back as soon as I can. There's no news excepting that this is leap year and horses ain't worth stealing no more."

It was signed "Uncle Bill" then left on the table with the sugar can to hold it down.

That done Uncle Bill looked thru the box where old Zeb kept some horse medicines with which he doctored up what bunged up trading horses he might get. He found some for sprains, gave his horse one good doctoring, smeared some other mixture on Kip's horse's ankles, then he came back to the cabin, and rummaging around outside he seen some pieces of rope hanging under the eaves there, picked out three good lengths, one stouter, and he handed the other two lengths to the kids which had followed him around, like in fear to lose sight of him again.

"Take them," he says. "I'll tie 'em so they'll do for hackamores till you get to your outfits. I'd loan you my saddle,

Scootie, but I'm thinking I'll sure need it to anchor the roan horse to on the way to the ranch."

The kids, in their excitement of first seeing the old cowboy that morning then watching him run the renegades and following him around afterwards, had forgot all about their saddles, and it never came to them that they would have to ride bareback until they got them again. They'd somehow never thought that their saddles being behind would give them away as to their losing their horses and having to hoof it all the way from there to the cabin as they had. They of a sudden realized that the old cowboy knowed all about that, and they felt anything but proud. If they'd been more experienced to the ways of range men they'd of knowed that Uncle Bill hadn't come to the cabin just by his guessing that they would be there, and that the only way he would of tried to find 'em would be by tracking 'em, which he had. As it was, he'd found their saddles laying out there on the long bench on the big flat and easy read by signs as to what all had happened, how they'd stayed there for the night, how and why they'd lost their horses, and he'd worried some as he'd followed their boot prints if the kids would follow the horse tracks. He'd hoped so, for the horse tracks headed for the closest water, and being that the old cowboy was afoot himself by then and hindered with leading a lame horse he couldn't of very well caught up with them if they'd went on and on some other way. He'd had to unsaddle his horse then and turn him loose, but he didn't want to do that unless he had to because the horse being used to the rough country as his home range would of went back and a long ways to get to water, and he also needed doctoring. So it pleased him to see that the kids stuck to their horses' tracks, and that relieved his mind a considerable, for he'd worried as to their thirst and hunger and weariness.

The kids looked at one another and then at Uncle Bill as he handed 'em the ropes, feeling sort of sheepish with their sudden realizing that he'd tracked 'em, knowed where their saddles was, that they'd lost their horses, and hoofed it in for the many miles. There was no pride that they'd found food and water, and their horses again, all by their own selves. Even the catching of the three renegades which saved Uncle Bill so much trouble in getting later and which pleased him a whole lot didn't come to their minds, they only felt guilty of letting something happen which they figured wouldn't happen with any good range hand, because he'd know.

But Uncle Bill soon cheered 'em up on that, and as he looked at their faces and understood by their looks, he grinned and only said:

"Too bad you youngsters will have to ride for a ways, but that'll only make you appreciate your saddles all the more. That happens to the best of us once in a while. Like one time, I . . . but I'll tell you about that some other time. Let's get started and drift."

He told the kids to first catch their horses, then from the ropes they tied on their necks he made a "hackamore"

146

(halter-like) to go over their heads, leaving one rein for the kids to guide 'em with. The kids let their horses out of the corral and tied 'em up alongside of the little bay, then Uncle Bill shook out a loop to catch another one of the renegades, it was the sorrel, and being that one wasn't broke to lead and hadn't had a rope on him only once, when he was branded, he naturally couldn't very easy be held if roped by the neck unless some turns around a corral post or the saddle horn could be taken, and the old cowboy didn't want to take the time to fool with him or break him to lead right then. So, when he threw his loop it spread in front of the sorrel as he run by and caught both of his front feet. Uncle Bill let the rope slip thru his hands a bit then and when he "sat down" (leaned against) on it the sorrel took a nose dive and sprawled out flat on the ground.

The sorrel was heavy and mighty active, and the old cowboy had to do some fast work so as to keep him from getting his feet under him and getting up again, but the old cowboy was well experienced to that work, and as the horse quit trying to get up for a spell and while getting his wind, he snared a hind foot with the slack of his rope and tied it with the two front ones. The sorrel was now tied down, and even tho he tried hard, he couldn't get up.

The sorrel being tied down to stay, he got the rope he'd brought from the cabin and tied a hackamore on his head, the same as he had on the kids' horses. Then, with another rope made of the hobbles which the kids had been carrying around their waists, he singled out one of Zeb's horses, a

The sorrel took a nose dive and sprawled out flat on the ground.

black which he figured he could walk up to. He cornered and caught him and then led him close by the sorrel's head, then he took the lead rope of the hackamore on the sorrel, raised his head up a little and tied the lead rope around the other horse's neck, leaving only about two feet of rope between the two horses' heads. They was "necked" (tied together).

Making sure that all knots would stay tied, Uncle Bill loosened the rope off the sorrel's feet to let him up. He got up afighting and at what held him, but he didn't fight so much when he seen that it was no human holding him but just another horse, and when that other horse begin to protect himself some and landed a few blows of his own, that sort of made the sorrel come to time. . . . He couldn't of been led but he could be drove, and being necked to Zeb's black horse he couldn't get away and would be about broke to lead by the time the ranch was reached. Well broke to lead alongside of a horse anyway.

Now there was only one more renegade to attend to, that was the big roan. Uncle Bill sort of wondered for a bit if to forefoot him and throw him as he did the sorrel or just catch him by the neck. He figured he'd be pretty hard to handle, even if he showed by saddle marks that he'd been rode a plenty. But he took a chance and flipped his loop over his head. The big roan snorted even before the loop lit on him, and when it drawed up around his neck is when Uncle Bill figured he sure had himself a wolf at the end of his string. The roan bellered like a mad bull and hit the end of the rope as tho it only made him peeved and sure wasn't meant to stop him. Uncle Bill skipped and hopped at his end of the rope and his pointed bootheels didn't touch the ground only at about every ten feet, but when they did they sure dug deep and the rope sang plum up to the roan's thick neck. It sort of stopped the big horse about every time the old cowboy sat down on the rope that way, but the roan was so big and powerful. . . . He sure knowed how to hit the end of a rope, he acted like he'd hit many and busted more than a few. Uncle Bill figured as much near as quick as the rope tightened around his neck, and then he wished he'd forefooted him, but it was too late now, and the only way he could get the rope off of him was to stop and hold him and get up to him.

As Uncle Bill planted his heels and jerked the rope tight on the roan's neck every time, that got to telling on the horse's wind. That old cowboy wasn't easy drug around, for he'd also been at his end of rope often in handling all kinds of horses, and had a way of flipping the slack at a right time so that when he sat down on the rope he near jerked the big roan to sitting down too. But there was no stopping or turning him like he'd done with some unbroke horses, sometimes even throwing 'em that way, and the roan didn't slow down for any time much until he'd come to the other horses as he'd run around the corral. It was at one of them times that the old cowboy figured on a sure way of stopping and holding him, and while the roan was mixing thru the other horses once more, he took a few feet of slack, run to the closest corral post and took a couple of turns around the bottom of it. He hoped that the rope and the post would hold, and to ease the strain, when the roan went to run on the rope once more he let the turns slip a little. That more than checked and surprised the horse, it turned him, and realizing that the rope was now around something that could hold him he went to rearing and striking at it and running one way and then another in trying to break it. But the rope was strong and near new and Uncle Bill had been lucky enough to pick on a good post in his hurry; it was deep in the ground and solid. The old cowboy had the ornery roan where he wanted him.

But it would take a little while before he would have him so he could come near him, for that horse was fanning the air with both front feet then turn to kick and run both ways on the end of the rope. As the horse kept afighting and running back and forth and leaving a little slack each time the old cowboy kept adrawing up on it until he had about half of the rope pulled in, and then the big horse begin to quit his fighting, he was getting winded, the rope was choking him and he begin to wobble. But he'd been in such a fix many times before and he was too wise to choke himself. He'd pull back in trying to break the rope and when his wind come short and he'd begin to wobble, he'd of a sudden come up afighting and Uncle Bill would have to do some dodging so as not to get pounded by his hoofs when he came up along the rope.

After each one of them spells the horse would then turn and hit to the end of the rope, always atrying to break it,

151

and sometimes he'd near throw himself when he came to the end so hard. Uncle Bill let him do that a few times, and then as the horse hit the end once more and come near throwing himself again, he figured on getting him that way. While the horse was sulking and getting his wind, the old cowboy gave more slack to the rope so that when he pulled back on it again, came up fighting and then run on the rope once more he'd have a *good* run. He also tied the rope that time and so it would slip a little when the horse hit the end of it.

Uncle Bill then went after him to scare him and pull back some more, the horse done that well and, as before, when he begin to run short of wind he let out a beller and came up on it afighting. The old cowboy had to do some more tall dodging to get out of his way, but when the horse went to hit the end of the rope this time he was right after him to spook him so he'd hit it all the harder. The big roan had plenty of speed when he hit the end that time, the rope slipped a little at the post and the kids could hear it sing as it stretched about two feet, and as the horse come to the end of it and bowed his neck the stretch of the rope was taken back while he was off his feet and he turned a regular made to order somerset, to lay stretched, and the wind knocked out of him.

As Uncle Bill had run after him to spook him, and expecting things to happen just as they did, he was on the big roan's head the second he fell. The horse had hit the end of the rope so hard and stretched it so much that when he was caught in the air and throwed he was sort of jerked back and there was slack in the rope. The old cowboy sure wasn't slow in taking advantage of that slack. Putting his weight on the horse's neck with his knees he twisted his head, nose up, loosened the loop from around his neck and, leaving it behind his ears, brought the hondo up to fit around his chin, part of it in his mouth. That made a "war bridle," and just what the big roan needed to make him come to time.

It didn't take Uncle Bill long to slap that onto him, just a couple of swift twists of the wrist and it was done, for with the loop and hondo the war bridle was already made, all he had to do was to fit it in place. It was good right then that Uncle Bill always tied a big hondo on his ropes, a brass hondo would of been useless, he'd never seen one, and he'd only laughed if he had.

The big horse had come out of his daze from the fall, and Uncle Bill was just thru with putting the war bridle in place when he started to fight to get up. He let him have his head then and the roan jumped up, ready to fight some more. But he didn't get to start at that much when the old cowboy gave the slack of the rope a light jerk, and that seemed to make the horse change his mind right sudden, for there was a different kind of a holt on him now, he'd run against that kind before and learned that that wouldn't get him nothing but pain, but there wouldn't be no pain if he behaved himself and led as he'd been broke to.

The war bridle is not a thing that should be put on a good behaving broke or unbroke horse. It's sometimes used on unbroke horses to break 'em to lead but a man has to use it easy then and he has to know how to do that or he'll mighty soon spoil a horse, make a fool out of him and will not break him to lead. There's very few men know how to handle a war bridle right on an unbroke horse and, as a rule, it's thought best not to use them. But with such outlaws as the big roan, the kind that's been broke, knows what they should and shouldn't do and then turn to be bad, jerk away from a rider if they can and go to play up all kinds of ornery tricks the war bridle is sometimes used, for them kind of horses get mighty rough, mean and tricky and they've got to be handled in ways according or nothing could be done with 'em.

The big roan, being wise to the war bridle, didn't fight it, and seeing that he'd better be good for a while he held his head up and stood, only snorting sort of quiet, and when Uncle Bill jerked on the rope just a little that big horse led up like a good one. His fighting was over, for the time.

The old cowboy untied the end of the rope from the corral post, led the big roan around the corral a bit to make sure of how he'd behave, and then, keeping back the sorrel and the black that was necked together, he told the kids to open the corral gate to the pasture and he let the rest of the horses run back out. The kids then led their horses and the little bay into the corral, closed the gate good and when the trap gate leading to the big flat would be opened they'd all be ready to line out.

Uncle Bill told the kids to get on their horses, that he'd be riding ahead and leading the roan and for the kids to drive the necked horses to following him and the roan. They would follow good once started, for driven horses take well to the lead of a rider, and being the black horse wouldn't try to get away he'd take to that lead in a short time, the sorrel would try to run and pull back and go in circles but he'd soon settle down to team along with the black.

"And I'll depend on you kids not to let them two get away," says the old cowboy to sort of make 'em feel happy at the responsibility, "but don't crowd 'em on me too much, just let 'em travel along at the same gait I take."

The kids got on their horses, they'd never rode bareback only for fun once in a while, but now they'd have a good spell of it. They was ready. They came close to the gate to keep the two necked horses back as Uncle Bill opened it. He opened and set it back, ready to be pulled closed again whenever old Zeb or anybody else would want to. Then he got on his little bay, and leading the roan he started on down the draw, looked back and told the kids to bring on their renegades.

The way out of the corral, down the draw to the big flat, was a natural run for horses to take to. Zeb's black might of wanted to hang back and stay by the good pasture but the wild sorrel necked to him hit for a run soon as he seen his way clear out of the corral. He wanted to follow the roan Uncle Bill was leading or hit out for the open flat, any place but away from the corral and riders. But the black

They now was headed for the ranch.

checked him up sudden on such ideas, and the sorrel only found himself circling back and forth in front of him and from one side to the other. There was no getting away, and the black's attentions was jerked away from the pasture as the sorrel yanked on his neck in trying to speed towards the big flat.

That way and as Uncle Bill had figured, the kids didn't have no trouble in keeping the two horses to following him and the roan. All they had to do was to turn 'em now and again from one side or the other and being they wasn't going fast that was easy to do. They had some fun watching the sorrel and the black, one wanting to go ahead so fast and the other hanging back, and as they rode along and all was going well they got some more fun out of their riding bareback, and what's more they now was headed for the ranch.

CHAPTER ELEVEN

KIP AND SCOOTIE was happy to be riding again. Their horses felt rested up and good under 'em, the two necked horses ahead of 'em made the riding all the more interesting, and then with the roan acting up once in awhile and Uncle Bill riding in the lead that all made things sort of complete. They looked over the big flat below 'em and to the rough hills acrost it, the same big flat and rough hills that had looked so bleak, desolate and treacherous only a couple of days before, and now they looked all friendly and cheerful and inviting.

As far as they was concerned they wasn't in no hurry to get back to the ranch, for the old cowboy was with them again and all was well. They'd enjoyed staying at the cabin for a few days and trap some more horses, putter around the cabin, and maybe get to meet old Zeb. With Uncle Bill that would all been a lot of fun.

But, with him, any place was a lot of fun, and interesting, and now, going back to the ranch it was with happy feelings that they followed his lead. . . . But the day was only well started.

On account of the kids riding bareback, Uncle Bill didn't travel fast, he kept the horses to a walk all he could and only broke into a trot when he had to, to keep the necked horses from passing him on one side or the other, for the sorrel was pulling steady on the black's neck and wanting to be on the run. The little bay the old cowboy was riding proved to be a fine little horse, wise to the rope on the roan that was being led, and seeming like ready to do his best at any thing that came up. The roan had tried a few tricks but Uncle Bill wasn't afraid of losing him, not while he was riding the little bay.

The sun had been warm as the outfit started out from the corral, and as mile after mile was covered on the way along the big flat it begin to get hot, too hot for comfort, and when Uncle Bill look back at the kids once in a while he noticed that they was beginning to squirm on their horses' bare backs. He'd laughed if it hadn't been for the distance they still had to ride that way, but as it was he sure wished they had their saddles. He didn't dare let either one of 'em have his saddle so as to relieve 'em. His saddle wouldn't of been much comfort to them anyway and he sure needed that horn on it to hold the roan which every once in a while would take a notion to run on the rope now and again and try to get away. The big flat sure called on all of his wild instinct, and now he wanted his freedom more than ever.

As they rode on and on, the kids soon enough got to the stage where they thought bareback riding was all misery and no fun at all. It might be all right for a mile or so, they figured, but for any further than that they'd sure want their saddles. They thought of walking and leading their

The roan had tried a few tricks.

horses once in a while but just about the time they'd decide to do that the two necked horses would begin trotting up, and being they couldn't of kept up with 'em afoot they stayed on their horses.

It seemed about twice the amount of hours than there really was before they got on the rise on the big flat and to where they could see the long bench where they'd left their saddles, and that long ridge still looked plenty far away. They felt not as tired but near as miserable as they did while on the last of their walk from their saddles to the cabin a couple of days before. Finally, and when their misery got to be too much they decided to walk a ways, regardless of the necked horses. They slid off their horses, but too fast, their legs buckled up under 'em and they sprawled down to the ground. They hadn't reckoned on their legs being numb and cramped.

They stayed sprawled for a spell, wondering, but the ground felt good. They looked at one another and laughed, and holding on the lead ropes of their horses they rolled in the shade of 'em and stretched. That felt near as good right then as if wading in a good swimming hole. Just to be able to stretch, the legs free and the back flat to the ground, was a great relief and sure pleasant.

Uncle Bill, looking back and seeing the kids off their horses, grinned a little. He knowed what was ailing 'em. He turned and rode to where they was stretched out.

"Sure solid comfort," he says, grinning down at 'em. "I should of thought and brought along a couple of feather mattresses and parasols."

"And a couple of ice cream sodas," Scootie added on, stretching some more.

"I'd be satisfied with just my saddle," says Kip, making a face as he reached for a rock that was digging into him.

"Well, it ain't so far to the saddles now," says Uncle Bill, looking towards the long ridge, "only about five miles, I should judge. (It was nearer twice that far.) But take your time and rest up all you want. I see the sorrel has quieted down now and him and the black are grazing, so they won't give us any trouble in trying to get away now."

"But we ought to be travelling as much as we can," says Kip, slowly getting up on his feet, "and I think walking for a change will do us good. When we get tired of that we can ride some more."

Scootie wasn't very anxious to be up and going so soon but, like Kip, she also figured they'd better be travelling all they could, then again, walking would limber her up. It would seem good.

So, telling the kids once more to stop and rest whenever they wanted to, Uncle Bill rode on to take the lead again. The necked horses took to following him and the roan as Kip and Scootie started walking a ways behind 'em, and they went slow enough so to nip at scattered tufts of grass as they trailed along.

Leading their two horses, the kids walked at a pretty good gait. The sun was beating down on 'em pretty hot but they felt better walking than they did riding, and even tho it was now past noon they wasn't feeling so thirsty as yet. They'd tanked up on all the water they could hold before leaving the corral. They felt that they could go a long ways, and now that the old cowboy was always in plain sight of 'em all would be well.

They walked until they got tired and to thinking that riding wouldn't go bad for a change, even bareback riding. They traveled a little faster then, and Uncle Bill, watching them, and knowing that they was anxious to get to their saddles, led on to as fast a gait as they seemed to want, sometimes to a trot and even to a lope for a ways. To make time, the kids traveled on as fast as they comfortably could while on their horses. Then, when riding got to be more then they could stand again they got off and walked some more.

It seemed a mighty long time getting to the long ridge, and at times it seemed like that ride was moving away from 'em. They changed from riding to walking a few times and then they come to their tracks of a couple of days before, just about where they'd found the second hobble. The kids looked at one another and now grinned at the thought of how they'd felt when they found that second hobble, but in their memory it wouldn't be so much to grin about.

From there they could about figure the distance to their saddles and that seemed to make it shorter. They changed from riding to walking once more, then got back on their horses again and when finally about a mile from where their saddles was they started to ride on a lope, that was easier on 'em and they would get to their saddles sooner. Uncle Bill grinned to himself and gave them plenty of lead, and

It seemed a mighty long time getting to the long ridge.

at last they come to the long ridge and then to sight of the saddle blanket covered shapes.

That looked mighty good to the kids and they wasn't slow in sliding off their horses and getting to their outfits. Uncle Bill, seeing that the two necked horses had stopped to graze, rode to join the kids and see if all was in shape. He was a little afraid that pack-rats or other range varmints might of begin chewing on 'em, but as the kids raised the saddle blankets and smoothed 'em on their horses' backs and then picked up their saddles there was no sign that anything had bothered 'em, but the old cowboy had noticed cayote tracks not far away from 'em, most likely only some inquisitive younger one, he thought.

There was some mighty happy looks on the kids' faces as they got in their saddles and was ready to ride again. Nobody could tell 'em about riding bareback any more, and anybody that wished to was welcome to all of that, as far as they was concerned, they'd stick to their saddles, well made stock saddles. They'd been pretty tired as they slid off their barebacked horses but now on the same horses but with their saddles on 'em they somehow felt rested up and at ease, and ready to ride on for a long ways.

All set, and the necked horses stirred from their grazing, Uncle Bill took to the lead again. He could now set any pace he wished, all excepting to maybe running renegades in the rough country. The rough country was to their left as they rode on, and the going from there on being new to the kids they wondered a lot as to the direction the old cowboy was taking, for they was still lost, and like when on the long ridge, they still didn't know which direction the ranch was, but the direction Uncle Bill was taking now was altogether wrong to them and the last one they'd taken. They'd went just the opposite direction and thru another part of the rough hills, figuring that the ranch was in that direction on the other side of 'em. It was a good thing they was now with the old cowboy or they'd got lost plenty more. They didn't realize that while trying to follow the old cowboy in their ramblings thru the rough hills they'd made near a half circle, and now they wouldn't have to go thru them again to get to the ranch. For as Uncle Bill was headed they'd travel on the big flat along the edge of the rough hills to a pass where them hills met up with the tall range of mountains which had been to the left of the kids as they'd walked to the cabin while following their horses' tracks. Now that same range of mountains was on their right, acrost the big flat valley, and at the foot of the same range of mountains, only beyond the pass Uncle Bill was now headed for was where the ranch layed.

The kids come near doubting the old cowboy's lead as they rode on, and a couple of times they'd about decided on riding up to him and asking him about that, but they knowed they'd only felt sheepish if they had and he'd only grinned at 'em and rode on. He'd always been right, and thinking of the way they'd got lost they felt foolish at doubting him. Anyhow, if they got lost some more they wouldn't mind it so much now because he would be along this time.

So they felt cheerful, even tho it was hot and they was getting a little tired and thirsty. As they rode on they looked at the big range of mountains to the right of 'em, watching for some familiar landmark, also at the rough hills, but what drawed their interest the most was the pass up ahead and which Uncle Bill was heading for so straight. They was anxious to see what was on the other side, and at the gait they was travelling now, at a good trot, the distance to it was being fast eaten up. They figured to be on the pass before very late that afternoon.

It was easy now to drift along. They kept the necked horses travelling and to following Uncle Bill in fine shape. The sorrel was now a well behaving horse and going along with whatever pace the black took, without a jerk either way, and as for the big roan he'd also quieted down to steady travelling and he'd quit trying to break away, but, as was his nature, he was always watching and would be quick to grab a chance to get away if one ever come. But he would never have no such a chance, not while Uncle Bill had a hold of him and while he was riding the little bay. That little horse showed no sign of tiring as yet, and as the old cowboy would of said about him: "He was a plum good one." As for Kip's and Scootie's horses they knowed where they was headed, to the next best place from their range, and coming right along, and, all in all, the outfit was sure getting somewhere, smooth and peaceful and at a good gait.

They rode right along and steady during the heat of the day, and it still wasn't getting any cooler when, getting close to the pass they come to a draw that led to a deep canyon up to the side of the mountains. Uncle Bill turned and led up that draw to where it narrowed, and there was a grove of quakers. At the sight of 'em the kids thought of water, the shade of 'em sure looked good, but they had to ride on a ways above the grove before they found water, and there was a ground tank full of it and running over. It was big enough so about fifty head of stock could drink at once, and by the side of it is where Uncle Bill stopped.

The horses was watered, and all having had their fill, was tied in the shade of a high rocky cliff, all but the two necked ones which stopped to graze close by. Uncle Bill then took a couple of packages from his saddle pockets, and with the kids went to the spring that kept the ground tank filled.

A clear little pool was there at the spring and fenced around so no stock would get into it, and crawling thru the fence, Uncle Bill and the kids rolled their hat brims to dip water with and drink out of. The old cowboy wasn't very thirsty and, while the kids dipped for more water, he begin to unwrap the two packages he'd took out of the saddle bags. They was the packages of grub which he'd had Martha fix up for the kids before leaving the ranch to go on their trail. He'd packed the grub in his saddle pockets all the way, and he'd went over a night and more than a day without anything to eat.

The grub, being wrapped in some kind of oiled paper, had kept good, and as Uncle Bill went to unwrapping he figured that it would be a good surprise for the kids. It *was* a very good surprise. They'd expected nothing to eat or drink till they got to the ranch, but their appetites didn't care what the brains thought, it was there and acalling. And now there was food to ease 'em, when not at all expected.

Martha's sandwiches and other things she'd fixed up went mighty well. Uncle Bill wasn't going to eat anything at first because he was used to only two meals a day and felt that he could easy go on till he got to the ranch, besides he wanted the kids to eat all they could and save the rest in case they got hungry again. But the kids wouldn't listen to that, and to please them he et a couple of the sandwiches, for, as they'd said, there was a lot more than they could get away with.

Being there was still a considerable ride to make before the ranch would be reached, the three didn't take much time to eat and they didn't linger long afterwards. It was nice and cool in the shade of the willows by the spring but, right then, they was anxious to drift on, for, as Uncle Bill had said, it would be about dark by the time they'd get to the ranch.

They got on their horses, Uncle Bill, leading the roan, went ahead once more. Kip and Scootie started the necked horses to follow and all filed along on plain trails leading to the pass. A good view of the big stretch of country they'd just come thru, they'd know it again and from any direction. But they was more anxious to see the country on the other side of the pass, and now that they was close to the top they made their horses walk a little faster.

It was a cowman's paradise.

Once on top and when they could see the whole country for many miles ahead of 'em, they stopped their horses. That country ahead looked very different from the country they'd just passed, a big flat fifteen miles long and wide, thick with green grass, trees here and there, and all sur-rounded with well timbered mountains. It was a cowman's paradise.

Kip and Scootie both pointed acrost the big flat, and both hollered at the same time.

"There's the cottonwoods. The ranch."

CHAPTER TWELVE

THERE WAS A WHOLE WEEK at the ranch when the kids didn't do much riding. It wasn't the needing of rest that kept 'em from riding as usual, for their first night back at the ranch to a late breakfast the next morning had set 'em up to as fine shape as ever. Martha had seen to all of that with a glad heart. . . . What had kept 'em from their usual riding and with Uncle Bill was a new interest which, for the time being, put riding and making pack trips in second place.

The new interest was that Kip and Scootie had thought of and decided to start a cow outfit of their own, that is, they was playing like they was, and they'd got so interested in doing that that they didn't have much time to ride, not for a starter and, as they'd said, until they got the outfit in running order and begin to get their big herds of cattle. First there was the "home ranch" to be built and as it ought to be, and there's where most of the whole week's time had went.

Not far from the corrals and sort of by itself from the big ranch house was an old abandoned two-room log house. It had been the first building on the Five Barb range and built by the kids' grandfather Powers when he first came and settled there, when the buffalo still roamed the big valley and the Indians paid no attention to their reservation lines. The big cottonwoods that now stood by the ranch buildings hadn't been planted for some years after that first house was built, there'd been no fences, and only one round corral.

There was still signs of the corral, and the old log house had settled mighty close to the ground but the lower logs had been layed on a few stones and was still sound and the ones above, being high and dry was also sound, they'd been dove-tailed well and the walls was still straight. But the heavy dirt roof had leaked and rotted the heavy ridge timbers holding it, and all had caved in and also rotted the flooring to the ground.

The kids had often noticed the old log house, and on account they'd been told that there was where their grandfather had first lived when he started the ranch, they'd nosed around it once in a while as they'd rode by. But the old house would of stayed and settled on as it had if it hadn't been for the kids' stay at old Zeb's cabin. And Kip, after him and Scootie had been back to the ranch a couple of days, riding along with her one day and seeing the old house, rode close to investigate it once more. He'd reared up as an idea came to him, and het up all at once on the idea he told it to Scootie.

The idea was to make a cow camp out of the old house, to clean it up inside, put another dirt roof on it, replace the doors and windows and floor and make it liveable. After that he was going to fix it all up just like Zeb's was and live in it. Scootie wasn't invited to have anything to do

It had been the first building on the Five Barb range.

with it, and at first she didn't care nor took any interest much, but as Kip meant what he'd said and proceeded to work and carry out his plans she begin to work along with him, and making plans of her own.

Kip had thought only of fixing up the old house to make a camp like old Zeb's and fix it up to suit himself that way and live there like in his own place, all but cooking his own meals. He'd included no lady's touch to it. But it was Scootie's idea, while making her own plans, to play at starting a cow outfit, her and Kip being pardners, and that way she would have some interest in the place. . . . Uncle Bill would be their foreman.

The idea went well with Kip and gave him still more interest in fixing up the old place. Being there was two rooms to it and that they was separated with a roofed-over space between, which had also collapsed they started on one room only. That would do, they thought, and as the work of clearing out old rotten timbers and dirt was started Kip naturally thought he was the main owner, Scootie also naturally figured she was about as much, but as that work was started there was no words or understanding as to that as yet.

Shovels and a wheel barrow had been brought down, and the two had went to work like real pioneers that had settled there for sure. They'd even kept their ponies hobbled or picketed close by in the tall grass, always handy for fear of the Indians.

Uncle Bill had grinned at their new interest and the way they'd went to work at rebuilding the old house. He'd

175

acted mighty proud and pleased when he was informed that he was foreman of the new outfit, they hadn't thought of a name for the outfit yet, and as the old cowboy done his riding most always by himself now he missed their company quite a bit. But he cheered himself some with the thought that with all the work they'd have to do to fix the place up they'd soon enough tire of that and lose interest. Once in a while, when his riding was over for the day he'd come and talk "old times" with 'em as they worked but he wouldn't help 'em much, for the old cowboy wasn't much for a hand when it came to any work where he'd have to get off his horse to do.

The whole week went by and the kids worked like beavers, they'd made quite a showing at cleaning up the old place, and they would soon be ready for new ridge logs and lumber to rebuild it. They showed no signs of losing interest, the old cowboy noticed, and he couldn't get 'em to come and ride with him unless the riding would be of special and thrilling kind, and he could hold 'em only for about half a day even at that, for they'd have to get back to building "and get settled before winter set in," as they'd say.

Then one day, in the middle of the afternoon, Scootie, happening to look away over the direction of the pass they'd come over about a week before and where the rough hills and mountains met, seen a long tall dust soaring up and slowly coming acrost the valley, and under it she seen a long dark ribbon of moving objects, it was a big herd of cattle.

She called Kip, and as the two looked at the long herd they come to figure for sure that there was a herd of their Uncle Frank's, and that him and his riders was driving it, maybe to some high range for the summer. At the sight of the long herd, which always causes any rider's blood to tingle, and with the thought of seeing their Uncle Frank and his riders again the kids of a sudden forgot about their pioneering and the starting of their cow outfit. . . . There was their herd coming in, Kip had said, laughing and excited, and their "home ranch" was yet without a roof.

They was watching the herd and wondering if to ride now and meet it or wait a while when they heard the sound of a loping horse coming behind 'em, and turning to look they seen it was Uncle Bill. He rode close to 'em, and grinning with pleasure the same as they was, he says:

"Well, pardners, there's the buffalo herd. Don't you think we ought to get a few to fill our larder before the snows come? We might have to shoot it out with the Indians that's chasing it but that'll only sharpen our appetites. . . . To your horses, men."

The kids wasn't slow in getting the meaning of the old cowboy's talk, and their horses and saddles being handy, as always, it didn't take 'em long to saddle and mount up. It was near as exciting to them as tho the herd really had been buffalo and the riders was warring Indians they'd have to shoot it out with.

"Leave big Chief Powers for me," says Scootie as she got on her horse.

The three started out on a lope. Kip rode to one side to the ranch house and, in regular Paul Revere style, hollered at Martha that the herd was coming, he then rode by the cook house and hollered the same at the cook so all pots for all hands would be started to cooking things, for it was getting late afternoon and the herd would most likely be held at the ranch for the night.

The herd was only a few miles away, and Uncle Bill and the kids loped along so that they was soon enough near it to recognize some of the riders. Uncle Frank was at the point of the herd and he rode out to meet them as the three headed for him, and he sure shook some of the trail dust off of him onto the kids as he met them.

"I should of left another man to take Uncle Bill's place and so he could of took you kids to the roundup," says Uncle Frank, as the three rode for the herd, "but I'm short handed this year and couldn't spare one man. . . . Well, I hope you had a good time since you got back anyway."

"We sure did," says Kip, and as he said that he sideglanced at Uncle Bill, hoping that old cowboy wouldn't say anything about their getting lost. . . . But neither Kip nor Scootie needed to worry about that, for Uncle Bill was sort of close mouthed in saying things where the saying don't help, either in a joking or a mean way.

The herd was drove and turned loose in a small tight fenced pasture where a creek run thru and close to the ranch. There'd be no guard for the riders to stand for that night and that'd be some relief as they'd been taking their shifts

Uncle Frank was at the point of the herd.

at standing night guard for near a month. The wagon loaded with bed rolls and other things necessary during roundup pulled in at the ranch before the herd did and was left by the bunk house, but not many, if any, of the bed rolls would be brought inside, for as used as the riders were to sleep under the sky, cloudy or starry, they'd felt might stuffy and like something would be weighing 'em down if sleeping under a roof, even if the door and all windows of the bunk house was wide open. Such a place is fine during winters, but for the time the beds would be unrolled on any level enough spot and left outside.

The saddle bunch had been brought into the corral, and as the cattle was left in the pasture and all riders went for the corrals to unsaddle, the kids was having the time of their lives mingling with all hands and talking of things of the summer before. There was only two riders which the kids didn't know but them two wouldn't be strangers for long.

At the corrals, the kids enjoyed everything, like all was a big holiday and celebration, the company and busy goings on with the cowboys unsaddling, their talk, saddles being layed on the ground, horses turned loose to enjoy a good roll in the corral dirt and then joining the saddle bunch, about fifty in all. A small remuda. A couple of the horses was roped to be kept up for the night and used to wrangle with in the morning, and then all the other horses was turned loose in a big pasture where they could graze thru the night without the "nighthawk" (night herder) disturbing 'em.

When that was done the riders hit for the bunk house where they would find a level spot to unroll their beds before night come, also to wash the day's dust off around their ears and eyes and then smoke and stretch out to wait until the cook played his tune on the triangle iron which served as a dinner gong. They wouldn't have long to wait, for, according to the sun it was near time for the evening meal, and being there'd been no noon meal that day the riders would sure be doing full justice to what the cook put on the table that evening. They hadn't et at a table for a month, and that would seem a little strange.

Uncle Frank and Uncle Bill, with the kids alongside of 'em, started for the ranch house, and being the two old hands was talking some of the works of the past month or so and since the last time they seen one another, the kids kept quiet and sort of held their jabbering until all gathered again at Martha's well loaded table. Then they broke loose, and with Martha joining in once in a while, it all made a reunion which lasted well past the kids' bed time, also the riders' bed time, for daybreak comes mighty early and the work with the day past and the day to come is never short for a cowboy.

The kids wasn't sleepy and they didn't want to go to bed when the time come, but they paid for that, for they overslept and when after they'd hurried to wash and thru their breakfast and run down to the corrals they found only their two horses there. All the riders, even Uncle Bill, had caught their horses, turned the rest out and rode away, and when they climbed up on the corral shed to look where the herd had been pastured they seen that herd strung out and about a mile away from it.

The kids could of course easy catch up with the herd but they sure didn't like the thought of being left behind napping. That sure wouldn't go well for a cowboy. If Uncle Bill hadn't left 'em it wouldn't of seemed so bad, but that old cowboy had done that just apurpose, for a joke like, and to sort of teach 'em to be on their own, also to hint that if they was to make hands of themselves they couldn't sleep on the job.

The kids kind of got that hint and they wasn't slow in catching up their horses, saddling 'em and riding for the herd. There was a couple of gates to open and close on the way and they sure begrudged taking the time of doing that, blaming themselves for oversleeping all the while, but when they loped up close to the herd they begin to put a bold and smiling front, like ready to take on or dodge any remarks they knowed would come their way for sleeping late.

There was a few come from the grinning riders, and as they rode on to the point of the herd and on the side where Uncle Bill was riding that old cowboy piled up on the remarks by saying:

"Well, little silver spoons, was the silk sheets hard to get out from between this morning?"

A little later and as they rode on the other side of the herd, Uncle Frank added on another remark.

"You sure must like your eggs hard boiled," he says. "And did you bring a few along? Because if you're coming along with us you're apt to get hungry. There won't be no noon bait and we won't turn back until this herd is well scattered up in the mountains. We won't get back to the ranch before sundown."

The kids thought that over for a spell as they rode along and decided to follow the herd, figuring they could turn back any time they wanted to. But time goes by well while driving a herd and it all was very interesting to the kids, seeing so many cattle, all ages and sizes awinding along in a string near a mile long. Then riding in the company of one joking rider and another all went to make time seem like no time.

There was over two thousand cattle in the herd, the way they was strung out the kids thought there was many times that number, and when they asked one of the cowboys how many cattle there was and he said twenty thousand, without blinking an eye, they believed him.

It was a little after noon, and the kids, forgetting about the time and not wanting to think about getting hungry, was still with the herd as it was getting near the mountains and left to drift a little as Frank and Uncle Bill, riding side by side, was talking about scattering the herd. The kids, riding near 'em, heard their Uncle Frank say as to how five hundred head would be shoved up to one place in the mountains, maybe eight hundred to another place, and so on till the two thousand head, the whole herd, was accounted for. When that was done and there didn't seem to be no more cattle to be accounted for, Kip, who'd added up the numbers in his mind as he'd heard 'em, pipes up and asks:

"Where are you going to put the other eighteen thousand, Uncle Frank?" . . .

Neither of the uncles dared open their mouths in answer to that, and they left Kip wondering as they rode on into the drifting herd, and Kip suspicioning something sure was wrong, started counting cattle as best as he could, just to get a rough count and an idea as to how many there *really* was. As Frank and Uncle Bill rode into the herd a few riders loped to the point and turned the leaders back, and then the herd was held. From the herd cattle was cut out by fours, tens and sometimes fifty in a bunch to where they was held out a ways by a rider, and when that "cut" (cut out bunch) counted to about the number that was wanted another cut was made, and another, until the herd was all divided up in four bunches, or small herds. Then two or three riders to each bunch they was started to wherever they was to be drove in the mountains to be left there to range. They would stay well up in the cool mountains and very little riding would need to be done to keep them from drifting to other ranges. But being them cattle was new to that range Frank would keep a couple of riders to ride line on 'em during that summer.

Frank and Uncle Bill, followed by Kip and Scootie, took the biggest bunch, the kids would sure be of some help. That bunch didn't have to be drove as far as the others but the way was steeper and the going would be slower. The kids worked well, and being there was many springs along the side of the mountains they didn't suffer from any thirst and they enjoyed the driving. The quaker groves here and there amongst the pines was mighty pretty and the riding thru the trees over pine needles or acrost clearings over tall green grass was mighty pleasant. Life on the range was sure great, the kids thought, while things was like that.

It was about middle afternoon when the cattle reached the top of the mountain and was drove into a good wide mountain meadow to graze, lick salt and water as they wished, with plenty of shade to lay down and rest close by and cool breezes to keep the flies away. There was many such meadows up on that mountain, some bigger and some smaller and all covered with a thick carpet of grass.

Frank and Uncle Bill watched the cattle for a while, it was all so peaceful and plenty-like to see, and as they watched, Frank begin to talk of his herds accumulating. How he'd have to shift 'em so as to get the best use of his range, also get some more range, like this mountain range which he'd got that year and which he'd just scattered the herd onto.

"Yep," he says, "the outfit has sure spread, and now it looks like I'll have to put on some more men, if I can only find some good ones. I'll have to have some more horses broke too, so we'll have to start on horse roundup right away, cut out all that's got the makings of a saddle horse and start breaking them so they'll do to work some this fall. I thought I'd have Whit and Max do the breaking of 'em. They're good men, and from what I think I can pick out they'll have plenty of bronks to keep 'em at breaking for all summer."

Frank turned to the kids who had been sitting on their horses close by and listening with all ears, very wide open ears.

"How would you like to go on horse round up?" he asks 'em.

The looks on their faces said aplenty, and before they could answer, Frank went on:

"And speaking of the outfit spreading, and with hiring more men, breaking strings of new horses, all to keep up with the accumulating herds and range holdings it looks like I'll have to start a 'wagon' (roundup outfit) of my own, with a regular remuda and all. I felt like I ought to done that for the last two years past and now, after I've thought it over well I've decided to start my roundup wagon and outfit that way for this fall, that'll be some more to prepare for this summer. . . . And maybe," he added on, joking now and looking at the kids, "Kip here would take the job wrangling, or as a flunky, helping the roundup cook."

Kip didn't brighten up as was expected at that, instead he looked a little downhearted, and he only said, "I'll most likely be on my way to school when the fall roundup starts."

Frank and Uncle Bill laughed, a little. "No, maybe not," says Frank, "I figure on starting my roundup wagon out pretty early, maybe by the first of August, because I'll be shifting some more herds by then and we'll need the outfit."

"But what job are you going to give me?" Scootie chips in before Kip could speak.

Frank rubbed his chin and not seeming of being able of thinking up something for her, Uncle Bill suggests:

"How would she be as cattle queen, Frank? . . . She could give orders as cattle queens are supposed to do and the cowboys would do as they durn please, as they do do. Besides she's got an outfit of her own started now and it'd be well to keep on the good side of her." He grinned, "and I'm her foreman now you know, and Kip's, too of course. . . . Yep."

The last part of the talk was well along joking ways but the first part which Frank had said about the outfit spreading, and having to put on more men and horses and a roundup wagon of his own so as to handle the outfit was very true and would mean a lot more work. All mighty interesting too, specially for the kids. There'd be the horse roundup (they'd try hard not to get lost this time), the corralling of many horses, cutting out many to be broke, the breaking of 'em which would be mighty interesting for the kids to watch, when they wasn't working on their "home ranch" which they sure planned on finishing up, then riding with Uncle Bill here and there and after that there'd be the cattle roundup and the moving of big herds. . . .

As the two uncles and two kids rode away from the mountain meadow and on down the mountain side, headed for the ranch, the kids had no thoughts for their appetites, for them thoughts had gone to jumping from one to another of them interesting things they'd heard their Uncle Frank talk about and which they would be on hand at, helping, doing and seeing during the summer, and adding them things up, if all that they had in mind was done there sure wouldn't be no time for sleeping nor eating. They had not one thought of school to mar their pleasure in their other thoughts, school was too far away to think about anyway, and as they rode thru the pines on down a breezy mountain ridge they seen nothing ahead but a mighty interesting, busy and happy summer, full of what all their little hearts desired.

The yip, yip and howl of a cayote was heard echoing thru the pines and from the canyon to one side of the high ridge, and that went well, very cheerful-like now and according with Kip's and Scootie's thoughts.